NECESSARY PERIL

TRIUMPH OVER ADVERSITY

LYNN SHANNON

NECESSARY PERIL

And these three remain: faith, hope, and love. But the greatest of these is love.

1 Corinthians 13

ONE

Her father was officially exonerated.

Sierra Lyons swallowed down the bile burning her throat as fear clamped like a vise around her lungs. With a shaking finger, she scrolled through the article detailing Oliver Patterson's victory on her phone. A Chicago jury had found him not guilty of murdering his business partner. The trial had played on the news for weeks. Oliver held himself out as a successful entrepreneur, but authorities suspected he was the leader of Blackstorm, a mafia-style organization involved in drugs, illegal weapons, and human trafficking. The FBI could never gather enough evidence to prove it though.

Sierra wasn't surprised. Her father was as slick as Teflon and as deadly as a rattlesnake.

Accompanying the article were several photographs. Oliver stood in front of the courthouse. His graying hair was slicked back from a face hardened by hatred and time. Flanking his side was his wife, Cece. Plastic surgery and Botox, aided by good genetics, made her appear thirty, although she was well into her fifties. She was dressed for court in a demure navy suit and pearls. If she was bothered by the accusations against her husband, it didn't show in the photographs.

It was difficult for Sierra to imagine her mother in Cece's position. Gwen had been a kind-hearted woman with a heart of gold. Initially, she hadn't realized the kind of man she'd married, and after discovering Oliver's true nature seven years into their marriage, it'd taken months to plan an escape. Sierra had been seven, her younger sister four, when their mother whisked them away in the middle of the night.

Moving to Texas, along with obtaining new identities, had shielded them from Oliver's reach. But it hadn't brought peace. Sierra's childhood had been one move after another, her mother constantly fearful. With good reason. The words her father had spoken from the time she could remember echoed in her ears.

Loyalty is everything. Never go against the family, my darling girl. Never.

A shudder rippled down her spine. Did her father have anything to do with the recent deaths of her sister and brother-in-law? It seemed unlikely. Lucy and Paul had been killed two weeks ago in a single-car accident on a rainy night while on their way home from an anniversary dinner. Law enforcement had assured Sierra there was nothing suspicious about the tragedy, but she'd been frightened enough to fall back on habits engrained since childhood. A go-bag was stashed in the closet in her house, another in a locker at the bus station. Just in case.

She glanced at the photograph of her father once more. She'd kept abreast of his movements since learning the truth about her family. Everything she'd read, everything her mother told her, confirmed what her gut already knew. Oliver would kill her, given the chance. She gripped her cell phone so tightly her knuckles turned white.

Stop. There's no way he knows where you are.

Jacqueline Patterson didn't exist anymore. She'd been replaced by Sierra Lyons, and for twenty years, the new ID had kept her safe. There was no reason to believe that wasn't the case anymore. She'd

2

lived in Austin for the last five years. If her father had located Sierra, he would've ordered his henchmen to murder her long ago.

Sierra took a deep breath to calm her nerves and clicked off the phone before climbing out of the car. Dusk had fallen hours ago. Exhaustion seeped into her muscles. Her nephew, Daniel, was asleep in the car seat. Plump cheeks curved toward a soft chin. A blue knitted cap was pulled low on his head, protecting him from the evening chill, and a blanket was wrapped around his small form. He looked blessedly peaceful. It was a rare occurrence. Daniel was a sweetheart but prone to colic, which is why Sierra had spent the last hour driving aimlessly. Car rides had a magical way of lulling the infant into sleep.

That parenting tip had come from an online mom group Sierra joined out of desperation after she became Daniel's sole guardian. Motherhood hadn't been on her radar. She'd never spent any significant time with babies before Daniel was born, and even then, her interactions were limited. After her sister and brother-in-law were killed, Sierra was thrust into an entirely new life.

An owl hooted overhead. The wind kicked up, rustling the budding leaves on the oak tree and scenting the air with early spring flowers. Sierra glanced at the dark house, debating her options. If she moved Daniel inside, she risked waking him. She could sit in the car, maybe catch a bit of rest herself, but it was past dinnertime, and she was starving. Her stomach growled in response to the thought.

She eased the rear car door open. Daniel didn't stir as Sierra reached around for the mechanism to release the carrier part of the car seat from the base. Now the hard part. She had to remove Daniel, carrier and all, from the vehicle without disturbing him. Yesterday, she'd failed. The result had been two solid hours of pacing, rocking, and tears—Daniel's and hers. Sierra sent up a silent prayer to the Lord, took a deep breath, and lifted the baby gently before slipping from the back seat.

Success. Relief slipped through her, releasing some of the tension knotting her neck muscles. Sierra didn't bother to grab the diaper bag that also served as her purse. It could stay in the vehicle for now. Using her hip, she gently shut the car door and then hurried up the walkway to the front door.

The inside of the house was dim. A lone bulb in the kitchen illuminated the mess scattered across the open living space. A pile of clean clothes sat on a couch cushion, the television remote was on the floor, and the kitchen table held a stack of unopened mail. Cleaning these days was a luxury. Juggling a newborn and overwhelming grief alongside her late sister's affairs hadn't been easy. Especially since she was doing it alone. Thankfully, her job as an accountant allowed Sierra to work from home.

She gingerly set Daniel on the living room carpet. The baby twitched inside the carrier, his eyes fluttering open, hands and feet moving under the blanket. Panic sent Sierra's heart skittering. She froze.

Please, don't wake up. Please, don't wake up.

Daniel settled back into sleep with a sigh, his rosebud mouth mimicking the movements of nursing. It brought a smile to Sierra's face even as her heart swelled. Sleepless nights, spit-up on her clothes, barely having time to take a shower...all of it paled in comparison to the love she had for this little boy. He'd captured her heart, and there wasn't anything Sierra wouldn't do for him. He was all the family she had left.

She glanced at her watch. With any luck, Daniel would sleep for another two hours. Long enough for her to catch a quick bite and a cat nap before his next feeding. She'd leave him in the carrier for the time being. He was comfortable and warm. Daniel also seemed to prefer the nestled embrace of the carrier to the wide expanse of his crib anyway.

Sierra went into the kitchen. Her cell phone vibrated and she glanced at the caller ID. It was her sister's probate lawyer, Adam

Nichols. Sierra answered the call, tucking the phone against her ear while taking the electric kettle to the sink. She wanted tea.

"I'm sorry to disturb you, Ms. Lyons, but there's been a mix-up here at the office and I thought you should know immediately." The older man's voice was clipped and to the point. Sierra envisioned him pacing the length of his office, the bookshelves behind him loaded down with legal reference novels. "I've located a personal letter addressed to you from your sister."

Sierra flipped off the faucet, certain she'd heard him incorrectly. "Excuse me?"

"I know this must be a shock. This is an inexcusable lapse on my part. My secretary was on personal leave when your sister dropped off the letter with implicit instructions to deliver it to you with the will. Unfortunately, it was misfiled by the temp working in my office at the time. I'm very sorry. We located the letter today, and I thought you should know immediately."

Her gaze shot to a photograph attached to the refrigerator with a magnet. Lucy was sitting in a hospital bed with newborn Daniel nestled in her arms. Her dark hair was pulled away from her face, her expression one of pure joy and love as she gazed down at her son. "When did my sister write the letter?"

"I can't say precisely, but it was about two weeks after Lucy and Paul finalized their wills and Daniel's guardianship," Adam said. "I'll be in the office first thing in the morning if you'd like to stop by and pick it up. Again, I'm very sorry for the confusion."

Sierra shared a goodbye with the lawyer and hung up. She tossed her phone on the counter. Her sister had written a letter? Why?

And did Sierra want to read it?

Tears sprang to her eyes at the thought of seeing her sister's handwriting. She blindly turned, gripped the handle of the fridge, and opened it with more force than necessary. Condiment bottles rattled in the door. Her stomach churned, the news of her father's exoneration and the crushing pain of losing her only sibling mingling together like a rolling thunderstorm. Cold air washed across her heated cheeks. She didn't feel like eating anymore. Still, she forced herself to grab a box of leftover takeout Chinese. The baby needed her. She had to be strong and keep putting one foot in front of the other for Daniel's sake.

The sound of bubbling water from the electric kettle drew Sierra from her thoughts. She shut the fridge door.

A man stood on the other side.

Sierra screamed. He shoved her and the takeout box dropped from her hand as she collided with the countertop. Pain rippled up her spine. In less time than it took to blink, the intruder was on her, his weight trapping Sierra between him and the cabinets. An unyielding arm wedged against her throat, choking the last of her breath from her lungs, and the barrel of a handgun pressed against the side of her cheekbone.

Sierra stilled. Shock and confusion gave way to icy fear as she stared into the man's face. He wasn't wearing a mask. She didn't recognize him, but the lack of concealment told Sierra all she needed to know.

He intended to kill her.

"Where is it?" A sneer twisted his lips, and his eyes were dark recesses, flat and cold. Evil poured from him, more terrifying than even the handgun pressed against her face. This man had murdered before. A professional.

Her father had found her. Sierra mentally berated herself for not trusting her own instincts, for relying on the police report about her sister's death. She wasted precious time, and now, the mistake could cost Sierra her life.

The attacker pressed the weapon harder against her cheekbone. "I asked you a question. Where are the files?"

Files? What files? Sierra had no idea what he was talking about. Her heart thrummed in her ears, faster than a hummingbird's wings. She tried to draw in a breath, but the arm at her throat and the weight of her attacker prevented it. Black spots danced in front of her vision. She clawed at his arm, but if her nails caused him any pain, it didn't register in his expression. How could she provide the answer he wanted if she passed out?

Maybe he didn't care. In fact, her struggles only seemed to amuse him. Her fist connected with his jaw and his ugly sneer turned even more predatory. The attacker pressed the weapon harder against her cheekbone and then turned toward someone else lurking in the mudroom. "Get the kid. I'll take care of her."

Daniel! No!

The blackness was closing in. Sierra's focus narrowed to the attacker's face and a tidbit of information from the self-defense course she'd taken cut through her panic.

She jabbed at his eyes.

The hitman howled in pain. The pressure against her throat vanished, and she sucked in a breath. The victory was short-lived. He reared up and blindly grabbed at her. "You'll pay for that!"

Sierra's body flew through the air as he tossed her like a rag doll. She collided with the opposite countertop, her flailing arms knocking over jars of sugar and flour. The glass shattered against the tile floor. A cry came from the other room. Daniel. Footsteps—the other hitman, no doubt returning to see what had caused his comrade to scream—raced toward the kitchen.

She couldn't let them take her nephew. Sierra drew in another shallow breath, her gaze landing on the electric kettle within reach. Glass crunched as the second intruder entered the kitchen.

Without giving herself time to second guess, Sierra grasped the kettle's plastic handle and spun, jabbing her thumb onto the button to pop open the top of the appliance. The men screamed as boiling water flew onto their faces and clothes.

She tossed the kettle at the closest one's head for good measure before spinning on her heel and racing for the living room. Daniel was still strapped in his carrier, mouth wide open, face red from his wails. Sierra scooped him up without missing a step, her attention locked on the front door. She paused only long enough to snag her keys from the rack next to the door. The sounds of the men screaming from the kitchen followed her out of the house and into the yard.

Get away, get away, get away.

The mantra played over and over again in her head. She nearly slipped on the pine needles covering the driveway while racing to her vehicle. Within seconds, she snapped Daniel's carrier into its base. The little boy's wails broke her heart, but there was no time to comfort him. Not if they were to survive.

Two hitmen meant more could be nearby. Her father could've placed a bounty on her head. Any number of criminals could be descending, each one of them determined to murder her to receive payment and Oliver's favor.

Help me, God.

It was the only prayer she could come up with between her bouncing, fear-driven thoughts. Sierra slid into the driver's seat. Her hands shook violently, and she dropped the keys. They clattered against the floorboard.

"No!" She frantically fumbled for them, her fingers brushing against the cold metal. She grabbed them, popping up from underneath the steering wheel.

A large, looming shadow appeared in the doorway of the house.

Sierra bit back a scream and jabbed the keys into the ignition. The engine turned over, just as the man raised his weapon. She shoved the car into gear and hit the gas.

Gunshots erupted, mingling with Daniel's cries.

TWO

Darkness surrounded Kyle Stewart as he approached the broken-down sedan on the side of the country road. Things didn't look good for the little Honda. Smoke poured from the hood, leaking from every crevice, visible in the headlights of Kyle's truck parked on the shoulder. Exhaustion tugged at his muscles—it'd been a long day on the ranch—and his stomach rumbled. He'd been on his way to Nelson's Diner for a late dinner when he spotted the stranded car and driver.

A baby's wail reached his ears. The little tyke was visible through the window, face screwed tight with fury and tiny hands balled into fists. How could something so small make so much noise? The child's distress only cemented Kyle's decision to stop and render aid. He quickened his steps. The tendons along his shin protested, the injury to his right leg a reminder of all he'd lost overseas.

He'd come home. His fiancée hadn't.

The Honda's driver side door flew open, and a woman shot out of the vehicle, canister in her hand, catching Kyle off-guard. The nozzle was pointed in his direction. Bear spray? Mace? Either way, he didn't want to find out. He took several steps back, shock reverberating through him, and raised his hands in the classic sign of surrender. "I'm here to help, ma'am..."

The last of his sentence died on his lips as the headlights illuminated her face. There was no mistaking the beautiful curve of her cheek, those full lips, or that cascade of black hair. A man never forgot his first sweetheart, even if it'd been over a decade since they'd last spoken. Kyle's jaw dropped in surprise. "Sierra? Sierra Lyons?"

She blinked, and then the hand holding the canister lowered. Her shoulders sagged. "Kyle. I didn't recognize you. It's been a long time." She swallowed hard and offered him a weak smile even as her gaze darted to the dark road behind him. "Sorry about the pepper spray. A girl can't be too careful."

"Of course." He didn't blame her one bit. Knoxville was a safer town than most, but there were vagrants nonetheless. Kyle lowered his hands. "I noticed the smoke coming from your hood and stopped to help. There aren't many people out this time of night."

Sierra opened the rear door of her vehicle and removed the crying infant. She bounced slightly, rocking side to side while attempting to wriggle a pacifier into the little one's mouth. It was strange to see her with a child. Like walking into a time warp.

It was also a punch to the gut. If life had worked out the way he'd planned, Kyle would be married with his own children. But God had seen differently. It was a bitter pill to swallow, and one he hadn't come to grips with yet. But none of that was Sierra's fault. Kyle pushed his own hurt aside to find happiness for his old friend. "You're a mom. Congrats."

The baby latched onto the pacifier and his wails stopped. Sierra kept rocking. She ignored his comment, wincing as she glanced at the hood of her Honda. "How bad do you think it is?"

"I can look and see."

"I'd be grateful." Her gaze shot up and down the empty street again. "I need to get back on the road."

"Sure thing. Let me grab a flashlight and toolkit from my truck."

He retrieved the items and then popped the hood of her vehicle. Sierra tucked the blanket more snuggly around the baby. The tenderness in her movements brought a smile to Kyle's face. "Adorable kid. What's his name?"

"Daniel." She cupped the baby's head in her hand and kept swaying. "He's not happy about being in the car seat for so long. Probably hungry. We've been on the road for a while. We just passed through the center of town when the car started smoking."

Kyle tilted his head. He hadn't seen or heard from Sierra since the night of their junior prom. She'd worn a gorgeous beaded gown the same shade of her eyes. They'd danced, hung out with their friends, and after driving her home, shared their first kiss under a sky full of stars. It'd been a perfect, magical night. And then...Sierra was gone. No warning. No explanation. One day her family was living down the road from his, the next they'd left town without so much as a forwarding address.

It'd been his first heartbreak. Not his last or even his worst, but losing Sierra had left an impression. "Are you visiting someone?"

"No, just passing through." Sierra offered him a tight smile. "I don't mean to be rude, Kyle, but the faster we figure out what's wrong with the car, the sooner I can get going. Can you double-time it?"

Okay, no small talk then. Kyle ignored the ridiculous pang of rejection that followed. He wasn't a foolish teenager, head over heels for the girl next door. Years in the military had worn any naivety out of him, leaving him battle-scarred and weary.

He unlatched the hood and then carefully examined the vehicle. Sierra hovered nearby, still rocking Daniel, but her gaze never stopped roaming. Nervous energy poured from her. It was enough to set Kyle's teeth on edge. He caught himself inspecting the dark country road for any headlights, but it remained empty. "Are you expecting someone?"

"No." She laughed lightly. "Sorry if I'm jittery. I've been living in

Austin for the last five years and I've forgotten how quiet the country-side is."

He had the weirdest feeling that Sierra was lying, but for the life of him, Kyle couldn't figure out why she would. Shaking it off, he turned his attention back to the car. "Your radiator is leaking. That's why the car overheated." He ran his finger over the hole in the hose. It wasn't jagged, like a crack formed over time would be. This damage was uncharacteristically smooth. Strange. "I know a mechanic in town who can tow it to his shop. He'll give you a fair price for repairs. Unless you have someone you'd like to call..."

"Is it that bad?" She bit her lip and juggled the baby. Once again, her gaze shifted behind Kyle to the empty road before settling back on him. She was as jumpy as a cat on a hot tin roof. "Is there any way you can fix it? I know it's a lot to ask, but you're good with cars. Remember when you fixed my beat-up Ford with chewing gum?"

The memory eked a smile from him, even as concern swirled in his stomach. Several minor cuts marred the delicate skin along Sierra's collarbone, as if she'd recently run into glass. No other bruises or marks were visible, but she was standing partly in the shadows. She wasn't wearing a wedding ring. Kyle ran his finger over the damaged hose again. Had it been cut?

"I can probably jerry-rig something for you." He lifted the flash-light higher to examine the interior of the car further. Nothing else appeared wrong. "It'll hold temporarily, but we need to wait for the car to cool down first. Is there someone you need to call? Let them know you'll be late?"

She licked her lips. "No. I don't need to call anyone." She clutched the baby closer to her. "How long before the car cools down enough for you to fix it?"

"About twenty or thirty minutes."

A set of headlights shone in the distance. Sierra stiffened.

Kyle narrowed his gaze. "Is something wrong?"

"I..." Sierra licked her lips and kept rocking the baby, her eyes locked on the approaching car. Kyle's hand drifted to the concealed weapon hidden at the small of his back. The vehicle on the road took the turn for the highway and Sierra visibly relaxed. She breathed out, the air in front of her face misting in the frosty night. "No, there's nothing wrong." She met his gaze and smiled, but it didn't erase the worry lines riding her forehead. "Other than my car breaking down on the side of the road."

"Right." The woman was definitely in some kind of trouble. But from what? Or whom? Kyle debated pushing her for answers but sensed it would only cause Sierra to dig in her heels. She'd been stubborn as a teenager and, even then, intensely private. "Just so you know, any repairs I make will only be temporary. If you intend to go somewhere far, you'll need to have the hose replaced."

"I understand, but I really need to get back on the road. I'll have someone take a look at it first thing tomorrow."

"Of course." Kyle released the hold on his concealed weapon and returned his attention back to the Honda. Internal senses tripping, he felt the edge of the radiator hose again, his fingers running along the smooth cut in the rubber. He released it and then his gaze drifted over the rest of the vehicle. A set of holes were punched in the grill. Kyle bent down to examine them and his blood turned to ice. Sierra's strange behavior suddenly made a lot more sense.

Bullet holes. There were bullet holes in her car.

He straightened, a hefty dose of protective anger rushing through his veins. What kind of person would take aim at a woman and child?

"Was someone shooting at you?" Kyle did his best to temper his tone. He didn't want to scare Sierra with the intensity of his anger.

Her face paled. "No, of course not. That's absurd." She laughed, but it came out high and tight. Unnatural. "Can you imagine? That would be enough to give me a heart attack."

Kyle rocked back on the heels of his cowboy boots. Now he knew for sure Sierra was lying. The wisest course of action would be to offer her a lift to the nearest gas station, call the police to report the bullet holes, and take himself home. He abhorred liars, and whatever Sierra was involved in could be illegal. Why else would she hide what was going on? But the baby in her arms gave him pause.

What if it wasn't illegal? What if she was running from the baby's father? It was a possibility. Which made this situation potentially volatile and dangerous. Out here, on the empty country road, they were far too visible. The first priority had to be getting Sierra and her child some place safe. Then Kyle could figure out the next steps.

He closed the hood of the Honda. "There's a great diner up the road from here. Why don't we grab a bite to eat while we wait for your car to cool down? I don't know about you, but I haven't had dinner yet." He flashed her a disarming smile. "It'll be more comfortable for Daniel too. You said he's hungry, right? It'll give you a chance to feed him."

Sierra glanced down at the baby in her arms. The little boy was frantically sucking on his pacifier, and he was bundled well against the cold, but the temperature was dropping by the second. Thunder rolled in the distance. A storm was heading their way, not too far off by Kyle's estimation. Sierra seemed to weigh her options for a moment and then sighed. "Okay, let's go."

A few moments later, with Sierra's guidance, Kyle had the baby's car seat base strapped securely in the rear seat of his extended cab pickup truck. He tossed the diaper bag on the floor board and then Sierra loaded Daniel's carrier. She climbed into the back seat. "I'll sit next to him, if you don't mind."

"Not at all." Kyle circled his vehicle and then hopped in. He fired up the engine. Country music softly crooned from the speakers. As he pulled onto the road, Sierra turned around to peer out the back window. The road was empty, but worry flattened the curve of her mouth.

She looked like a woman with the weight of the world on her shoulders.

And Kyle was determined to find out why.

THREE

Sierra glanced through the rear window as Kyle pulled into the parking lot of Nelson's Diner. From what she could tell, no one had followed them. But how long would it take for the hitmen to discover her vehicle? Her Honda was only two miles away. There weren't many establishments on this country road. A couple of gas stations, a closed pet store, and two restaurants—a fast-food burger place and the diner.

Kyle's truck bounced over a pothole. An old-fashioned neon sign over the door glowed, the *e* from Nelson's flickering as if it was about to burn out. Crooked blinds hung in the windows. The air was scented with fried onions and grease. Sierra's stomach rumbled, reminding her she hadn't had dinner. But how could she possibly eat with a thousand worries racing through her mind?

Had she made a mistake by getting in Kyle's truck?

He parked and exited the vehicle. Time had changed him. His hair was shorn close to the scalp on the sides but left longer on top. The look exaggerated the sharp edges of his handsome features. His shoulders were broader than she remembered, and he was sporting at least fifteen pounds more than he had in high school—all of it muscle.

Sierra's heart skipped a beat as a dormant attraction for her teenage crush flared to life.

They'd been friends in high school, but Sierra had avoided getting close to Kyle. To anyone, really. It was hard to build genuine friendships when everything about her was a lie. Shallow relationships were safer. Easier.

Even at the tender age of sixteen, Sierra had sensed Kyle didn't do shallow. No, he was dangerous. The kind of man who'd wriggle his way past her defenses and into her heart. But she couldn't resist accepting his invitation to their junior prom. Nor could she let the wonderful night end without one sweet kiss.

Their brief romance had been cut short when Sierra and her family left town in the middle of the night. Her mother had sensed someone following her in the grocery store. It'd been enough to set them on the run again.

Cold air whispered across her face when Kyle opened the passenger side door. A smile played across his face, but didn't quite reach his eyes. "I know the place doesn't look like much, but I promise the food is fantastic."

Sierra hesitated. What was she doing? If the gunmen found them, it would put Kyle—and maybe others—at risk. Her gaze once again shot to the country road. Empty. She bit her lip, her stomach in knots, indecision warring within her. Maybe the attackers would never come across her vehicle. Sierra had specifically avoided the highway as she fled Austin hoping to throw them off her tail.

Daniel spit out the pacifier and gave a hearty wail. A quick glance at her watch confirmed it was feeding time. He would need a diaper change, too, all of which would be easier in the diner. There was no sign of danger at the moment, and hopefully, it would stay that way. They'd spend twenty minutes in the diner and then Kyle would repair her vehicle. She'd be back on the road in no time.

Decision made, Sierra lifted Daniel from the car seat, shushing him with words of comfort. Then she slid her palm into Kyle's. A rush of unexpected warmth traveled up her arm as his strong fingers gently closed over hers. He helped her climb out of the vehicle and then released her to retrieve the diaper bag. Unnerved by her reaction to his touch, Sierra distracted herself by wiggling the pacifier back into Daniel's mouth. "Hold on, little one. Food is coming."

The baby latched onto the pacifier, his mouth working overtime. Kyle shut the vehicle door and hit a button on his fob to lock it. "Let's get out of this cold."

Together, they crossed the parking lot. The low murmur of voices mingled with a mixture of scents inside the diner. A long glass display sat next to the register up front. Rows of mouthwatering pies sent Sierra's hunger pains into overdrive. The flaky crusts were baked to perfection, and since customers could buy by the slice, some fillings were visible. Every single one looked amazing.

"Best pie in Texas," Kyle said, before greeting the woman headed their way. "Hi, Harriet. Table for two." He paused. "Well, maybe two and a half."

Harriet laughed, her cheeks bunching with the effort. Her gray hair was tucked into a bun at the top of her head and a pair of reading glasses dangled from a chain around her neck. Her twinkling eyes settled on Daniel, nestled in Sierra's arms. "What a sweet baby. How old is he? One month? Two?"

"Six weeks tomorrow."

Harriet's expression turned sympathetic. "Ah, darlin, you're still in the thick of those middle-of-the-night feedings. It gets better, I promise." She snagged a set of menus from the counter. "Follow me. Want your usual table, Kyle?"

"If you don't mind, ma'am."

The table was nestled in a quiet corner next to a large window overlooking the parking lot. Some of the tension left Sierra's shoulders. She'd be able to see anyone coming their way. Within ten minutes, Harriet had gotten their drinks, taken the food order, and filled Daniel's bottle with warm, distilled water. It was obvious from the way she interacted with Kyle that he was a frequent patron. Once Harriet walked away, Sierra glanced at the pie display in between measuring spoonfuls of powdered formula. "Which dessert is the best?"

"My favorite is pecan, but you can't go wrong with any of them." Kyle leaned back in his chair. "Like I said earlier, the food here is amazing. Harriet and Nelson—the owners—make everything from scratch."

His gaze felt heavy on Sierra as she shook the bottle and then slipped the nipple between Daniel's lips. The baby latched on immediately, his attention fixed on her face. The magnitude of the attack she'd survived less than an hour ago slammed into her. What would've happened to Daniel if Sierra had been killed? She was all he had. Her fingers trembled, and she gripped the bottle tighter.

Kyle cleared his throat. "Hey, are you okay?"

She swallowed the fear threatening to close her throat and nodded. "Sorry. It's been a long day." A tear trickled down her cheek, and she swiped at it, embarrassment heating her cheeks. Sierra couldn't possibly tell Kyle the truth about why she was crying. At least, not the whole truth. But there was something she could say to explain her runaway emotions. "Daniel isn't my son. He's my nephew. My sister and brother-in-law were killed two weeks ago in a car accident." Sierra took a deep breath and read-justed the baby's bottle so he could get more formula. "My mom died a few years ago, so Lucy was all the family I had left. Now...Daniel is."

She swiped at another tear. Kyle pulled a napkin from the dispenser and handed it to her. "That's rough, Sierra. I'm sorry." His gaze dropped to the baby before lifting back to hers. "If it counts for anything, you're doing a great job."

She laughed despite herself. "You must be easily impressed." An awkward silence settled between them. Sierra sensed Kyle was calculating how to ask about the bullet holes in her car again. She needed to distract him. "Enough about me. How have you been since we saw each other last?"

"I went to college in Houston and then joined the Army. Got out about two years ago. Now I'm working on my family's ranch. What about you?"

"I went to college in Austin, fell in love with the city, and then stayed to work. I'm an accountant. Freelance. Running my own business is hard, but I like the freedom it gives me." Sierra pried the bottle away from Daniel and then raised the baby to her shoulder to burp him. "It's been especially helpful these last few weeks with Daniel. How are your parents?"

"They're fine. Thanks for asking."

Kyle looked like he was about to ask her another question when Harriet arrived with the food. Burger for him, meat loaf for Sierra. She finished feeding Daniel first, who fell asleep in her arms. She carefully balanced him in one arm and ate with the other hand. She swiped her fork through the creamy mashed potatoes. "Wow, these are amazing. You were right. How did you find out about this place?"

Kyle explained about his weekly dinners with a group of veteran friends. Sierra split her attention between him, Daniel, and the parking lot. She barely tasted the meat loaf or the veggies while she peppered Kyle with questions to keep the conversation light and moving. Every minute spent in the diner grated on her nerves. She was desperate to put as much distance as possible between her and the hitmen.

Once the last bite of food was eaten, Sierra reached for her wallet. "I'll pay and we can get out of here. I'm sure the car has cooled down by now."

"I don't think it's wise to go anywhere near that car." Kyle arched a brow. "Not until you explain to me where the bullet holes came from."

She froze and then forced a laugh. "What are you talking about? I told you, those aren't bullet holes."

He snorted. "I've been deployed to war zones, Sierra. I know exactly what bullet holes in a vehicle look like." He met her gaze, his dark eyes pinning her in place. "And I know you're in some kind of trouble. You've been watching the parking lot as though you're expecting the boogie man to pop out of the shadows."

Her cheeks heated. How had he been able to so easily see through her? Sierra had spent decades lying about who she was. She'd become skilled at hiding her emotions and avoiding questions. Clearly, the attack coupled with weeks of sleepless nights, thanks to Daniel, had worn down her ability to pretend everything was okay.

Kyle reached across the table and placed a hand on her arm. "You're scared, Sierra. I can see that much. Tell me what's going on. Maybe I can help."

His palm was warm enough to feel through the fabric of her shirt-sleeve. His grip was strong yet gentle and the concern in his expression...heavens, it was almost too much for her. Sierra was a strong woman. Tough. But the last few weeks had put her through an emotional wringer. Losing her sister, becoming a single parent overnight, and now hitmen threatening to kill her. It was overwhelming. A part of her—a big part—wanted to blurt out the whole truth to this handsome veteran who had once been her friend.

But she couldn't. This wasn't Kyle's problem, and telling him the truth only put him in danger. Just being with him at this table put him at risk.

Sierra forced a bright smile and pulled her arm away. "I don't know what you're talking about. I'm fine, Kyle. I'm not scared, just tired. Promise."

He scanned her face, and for a moment, she thought he would challenge her. Then the tension in his shoulders dropped. "Okay. Let's get moving then."

He waved Harriet over and asked for the bill. Sierra scooped it up. "It's on me. It's the least I can do."

Kyle shook his head. "Not a chance, Sierra."

"Please. It'll..." Movement in the parking lot caught her attention. A dark-colored sedan pulled into a spot close to the entrance. Two men in suits exited the vehicle. Neither of them was the attacker from her house, but Sierra's heart skipped a beat anyway. She knew them. Evan Rodriguez and George Sampson. They worked for her father.

The meat loaf in her stomach turned into a rock as the men assessed the parking lot. Evan was dark-haired and tall with a jagged scar near his temple. George was blond, short, and stocky. They both wore designer suits and stylish shoes. To the average person, they looked like businessmen in search of dinner after a long day at the office. But Sierra knew better. They were dangerous killers.

She jolted from her chair so quickly it fell back and clattered against the tile floor. Harriet stepped back in surprise. "Goodness, hon."

Sierra scooped up Daniel's diaper bag without taking her gaze from the men. They were making their way to the entrance. She couldn't allow them to see her. Without meeting Kyle's gaze, she muttered, "Excuse me, the baby needs to be changed."

She spun and bolted for the bathroom. There had to be an emergency exit nearby, right? Most places had one near the rear. But when she entered the small hallway in the back, Sierra discovered it was a dead end. Panic welled in her chest. She turned and ran smack into Kyle's broad chest. "Oh."

He lightly grabbed her upper arm to keep her from falling back. "Are those men looking for you?"

Denial wouldn't help her. Things had escalated beyond that now. "Yes. Where's the exit? I need to get out of here." Sierra swallowed down the lump of fear clawing her insides. "Quickly, Kyle. My life depends on it."

FOUR

"Come with me."

Kyle kept hold of Sierra's arm as he gently tugged her away from the bathroom and around the rear wall of the diner. His mind calculated different options with every step. Heading out the back exit could be dangerous. There was no telling how many men were searching for Sierra.

Five seconds. That's how long it would take for the men to reach the entrance to the diner. One was dark-haired with the muscular strength of a boxer, the other shorter and bull-necked. Each wore an expensive suit, but underneath the jackets, the outline of handguns were visible. They meant business. Sierra hadn't been exaggerating the threat to her life.

A swinging door led to the kitchen. Out of the corner of his eye, Kyle spotted Harriet moving in the same direction. Their strange behavior had caught her notice. The dark-haired man paused outside the entrance of the diner, his gaze sweeping across the guests visible through the window. His expression was flat and cold. Hard. It sent a chill down Kyle's spine.

He didn't know what was going on, but he wouldn't allow those men to harm Sierra or Daniel. Not on his watch.

Kyle barreled through the swinging door. Nelson, the owner, spun from his place at the stove. A chef's hat covered his bald head and stains marched across the front of his apron. Kyle kept hold of Sierra but was careful to keep his grip gentle. "We need a place to hide."

Nelson, God bless him, sprang into action without question. He hurried to a door on the far side of the room and unlocked it with a key. An office. It was small, a scratched wooden desk and metal filing cabinet taking up most of the space.

Kyle steered Sierra inside. Her complexion was as white as the flour sprinkling the tile floor. Somewhere deep inside, a mixture of emotions threatened to bubble up. Anger at Sierra's refusal to be honest warred with the ridiculous desire to comfort her and ease the worry lines from her brow. Neither would do any good.

Sierra dug in her heels and refused to enter the office. "I need to get out of here."

"We don't know how many men are here. Can you guarantee someone isn't watching the back exit, waiting for you to slip out?"

Sierra's mouth dropped open and then closed again. A new fear flickered in her eyes as she gripped Kyle's hand. "Don't confront them. Evan and George are dangerous men. You can't understand how much."

What on earth was going on? A million questions crowded his mind, but there was no time to ask them all. "Which one is Evan? The dark-haired one?"

She nodded. Kyle gently pushed her into the office. "I won't confront them if it can be helped. Stay here. And keep Daniel quiet if you can."

Harriet bustled into the kitchen. "What's going on?"

"Those men—" Kyle jerked his chin toward the diner entrance as

23

he closed the office door. "—are looking for Sierra. They can't know she's here."

Harriet's brows arched and the concerned lines bracketing Nelson's mouth deepened, but the couple didn't waste time asking for further information. Kyle was grateful they took him at his word. After leaving the military, he and several of his fellow veterans formed a support group. They met every Wednesday night at the diner. Over time, the older couple had become like a surrogate set of grandparents to all of them.

The bell placed at the front counter for customers to request assistance rang out. The wall separating the kitchen from the rest of the diner had a cutout designed to allow plates of food to be passed through. Kyle used the opening to study the men.

One of the waitresses was beelining for the counter but didn't move fast enough for Evan's liking. He hit the bell again as George meandered through the restaurant toward the bathrooms. His eagle-eyed gaze swept across the patrons seated at the interior tables along the way.

Sierra's warning echoed through Kyle's mind. If he spoke to the men, it would be conspicuous. It was far better to pretend everything was normal. Harriet seemed to come to the same conclusion. She straightened her shoulders and lifted her chin. "I'll take care of them."

The cutout provided a clear view of the cash register and front counter. Harriet's shoes squeaked against the floor as she headed toward Evan, waving off her waitress along the way. The woman diverted to another table full of customers. Kyle breathed out a sigh of relief. He couldn't swear the waitress wouldn't give Sierra away.

Nelson flicked the flame on the stove off and slid next to Kyle, his dark gaze following his wife. "What kind of trouble are we dealing with?"

"I'm not sure." Frustration nipped at him. He was running blind and didn't like it. How far would Evan and George go to get their hands on Sierra? The diner was full of innocent people, and while it seemed inconceivable the men would attack with so many witnesses, desperation could create terrible situations.

His fingers brushed against the handgun holstered at the small of his back. George rejoined Evan, shaking his head slightly to indicate he hadn't located Sierra. At the front counter, Harriet reached for some menus, a pleasant smile on her face. "How can I help you gentlemen? Table for two?"

"No, ma'am." Evan's voice was smooth with a hint of an accent Kyle couldn't place. "I'm looking for my sister. Her car broke down and she needs help. She called me from the road, but her cell was dying. I thought maybe she came in here."

"Afraid not. Have you tried the gas station up a'ways? That would be the first place I'd head to."

"I did, but she wasn't there." Evan removed his cell phone from his pocket and tapped the screen. When he turned it to face Harriet, Kyle caught a glimpse of Sierra's picture on the screen. "This is her. Maybe she was in here earlier? Sierra has a baby and I'm sure she walked someplace to get warm and charge her phone. I'm worried about them."

"I don't blame you. It's chilly tonight." Harriett's brow creased. "But I'm sorry to say she didn't come in here. I'll keep a look out for her though. If you leave me your phone number, I'll call if I spot her."

Evan didn't miss a beat. "That would be wonderful." He recited his number and then watched as Harriet scribbled it down. Then his attention drifted toward the kitchen. Kyle was hidden in the shadows, but his heart skipped a beat as Evan's gaze narrowed. "I'd like to ask the other customers if they've seen my sister. Maybe someone noticed her on the road."

"No need." Harriet answered smoothly. "People are chatty in these parts. A woman and a baby walking on the side of the road would've caught some attention, and I'd hear about it." She kept her expression and tone pleasant. "You might try the places closer to the freeway. Someone may have given her a lift there on their way out of town. There's a big truck stop and a couple fast-food places."

For one heart-stopping moment, it seemed Evan was weighing his options. If the men insisted on showing Sierra's picture to the other customers, it was only a matter of time before someone remembered seeing her. Kyle eyed the rear exit and calculated his options. None of them were good.

Evan flicked off his cell phone and returned it to his pocket. "Thank you for the suggestions, ma'am. And please, if you spot my sister, give me a call."

Harriet nodded. "Sure thing."

Kyle let go of the breath he was holding when Evan and George exited the diner. He waited until they'd climbed back into the vehicle and drove away before crossing the kitchen to the closed office door. Sierra was crouched behind the desk, Daniel attached to her chest in some kind of wrap. She held a pair of scissors in one hand as a makeshift weapon. The fear etched across her beautiful features was like a gut punch.

"They're gone." Kyle turned and caught Nelson's eye. The older man nodded in reply to his silent question—he would keep watch while they talked. Kyle closed the office door before turning his attention back to Sierra. He crossed his arms over his chest. "I think it's time you start explaining what's going on."

Sierra rose from behind the desk. She set the scissors down, and for a brief moment, was quiet. Then she sighed. "I was attacked in my home earlier this evening by two men attempting to kill me. I managed to escape, but one of the bullets must've hit my car, which caused the damage."

"Then we should call the police."

"No!" Her voice rose in a panic. "We can't involve the police. They can't help me."

Suspicion narrowed his gaze. "Why not?"

"Because..." She seemed to wrestle with some internal decision and then swallowed hard. Her hand came up to rest on Daniel's back in an absent gesture of protection. "The man who hired those thugs is extremely dangerous. He's the head of a criminal organization. They've bought police officers off before. I can't trust anyone."

Uncertainty stilled Kyle's tongue. He studied the woman in front of him, a former classmate who was little more than a stranger, and tried to suss out his feelings. Did he believe her? Kyle wasn't sure. Sierra had already lied to him several times tonight with ease. She could be a criminal on the run weaving a new tale of half-truths to garner his sympathy. "Sierra, if you've done something illegal—"

"I haven't." Her tone was indignant and her eyes flashed with anger. "I understand my story sounds bizarre, but I promise you, I haven't broken the law."

He wanted to believe her. The Sierra he'd once known had been kind and warm-hearted. Even now, the cross dangling from her necklace was a reminder of the things they'd shared, faith in God being one of them. "If you aren't involved in something illegal, then why does this criminal want you dead?"

"I'm sorry, Kyle. I wish I could tell you more, but it's safer if I don't. I appreciate all that you've done. Truly." Sierra's expression hardened. "But the best thing would be to repair my car as fast as possible and get back on the road so I can put some distance between myself and those men."

"Those men are professionals." Kyle's gaze dropped to the baby swaddled against Sierra's chest. No matter what he thought about her story, there was an innocent life at stake. That wasn't something he could ignore. "Chances are, they've left someone to watch your car." It's what he would do in their situation. "You can't go back there."

She didn't reply, but the crease between her brows gave away her thoughts. She hadn't considered that possibility. If she had a plan, it wasn't a good one. Kyle had doubts about her story, but the danger she was facing was all too real. And it was obvious she was woefully unprepared to handle it.

He was done with this game. It was time for some hard truths. "If you think you can outrun them, on your own, with a baby, then you're delusional. You need help, Sierra. That's something I can provide. You can stay on my family's ranch tonight, and then tomorrow morning, we'll figure out the next steps."

She immediately shook her head. "I don't want to put your family in danger."

Interesting. Her comment lent some credence to the tale she'd woven and quieted the screaming voice inside his head that warned him against inviting a potential criminal onto his property. "My parents are visiting my aunt in Waco. They won't be back until tomorrow. My ranch is the best place for you to hide out for the night. We haven't seen each other in over a decade, Sierra. There's no way the men searching for you will ever think to connect us."

"What about Harriet? And her husband?"

"They won't say a word to anyone." He bent down and picked up the discarded diaper bag from the floor. "You look tired enough to fall asleep on your feet. A night of good rest will help you think more clearly about what steps to take tomorrow morning."

She hesitated. Kyle held his breath, silently willing her to agree. For her sake.

And the baby's.

FIVE

She was drifting from one bad idea to the next like a branch caught in a tornado.

Sierra clasped her hands together in her lap, praying she was making the right decision by coming to Kyle's ranch. It'd been forty minutes since they left the diner, but her heart rate still hadn't returned to normal. Daniel squirmed in his car seat, sending out a mewling cry. Sierra wriggled the pacifier between his lips and he clamped down on it. His gaze never left her face. She stroked his soft cheek and, despite the desperate situation they were in, smiled. "We're almost there, Daniel."

She glanced up and caught Kyle's gaze in the rearview mirror. "We are almost there, right?"

He nodded. "I took a longer route home from the diner. Just in case."

In case they were followed. The very thought twisted her insides. Once again, she questioned the wisdom of going to Kyle's ranch. But what other option did she have? Oliver's men had found her, and Kyle's warning at the diner had been wise. These men were professionals. They were probably watching her car and her home in

Austin. She couldn't call any of her friends or colleagues. Once Oliver uncovered her secret identity, he'd track all the people closest to her. Not that she had many.

Meeting Kyle on the side of the road was divine providence. Or so she wanted to believe.

One night. Sierra needed time to plan her next steps, and with Daniel to care for, every decision had to be thought out. She mentally berated herself for not leaving the moment her sister was killed. Her mother, God rest her soul, would be horrified. She'd drilled into both of her girls the importance of constantly looking over your shoulder, never letting down your guard, and being prepared to run at a moment's notice. Suspicion had been part of their everyday lives. It'd been a difficult way to navigate her tumultuous teenage years, and even though she understood it, a part of her resented it as well.

She wanted to be normal. But there was nothing normal about her father being a cold-blooded killer and the leader of one of the biggest organized crime rings in the United States. Sharing DNA with that kind of person...it changed everything about her. Faith had been the only thing to pull her through. God knew everything about her. He saw through the lies she was forced to tell—about her name, her birthday, her family—and into her heart.

Deep down, Sierra knew she was a good person, but every falsehood chipped away at her conscience. She hated knowing she was a liar. It'd interfered with every relationship she tried to build. How could Sierra ever fall in love or have a best friend when she couldn't tell them the truth about herself?

It made the loss of her sister, Lucy, all that more painful. They'd been incredibly close. Relied on each other. Sierra's eyes pricked with fresh tears and she battled them back. Grief would have to wait. Daniel needed her now more than ever, and there was *nothing* Sierra wouldn't do to protect her baby sister's son.

Kyle cleared his throat. "We're here."

His headlights illuminated an arched gate with the words White

Oak Ranch stamped on the metal. The truck bounced over a cattle guard, and then moments later the trees parted, revealing the house. Made of stone and wood, it had a wide wraparound porch. Rocking chairs swayed slightly in the breeze. LED lights brightened the walkway and flower beds packed with gorgeous blooms. In the distance were several buildings, including a barn. Sierra had been to the property a few times as a teenager. The place was as beautiful as she remembered.

For the first time since the initial attack at her house, the tension eased from Sierra's spine. She sagged against the seat. Maybe it was a false sense of security, but she inexplicably felt safe here. Or maybe it was the man she was with. Kyle's quick action and rational line of thinking in the diner had saved her life.

He hadn't asked any questions, to her relief, since leaving the diner. Still, Sierra had the sense Kyle didn't believe her story. It hadn't stopped him from offering her a place to stay though. Why was he helping her? For a moment, Sierra considered asking, but then rejected the thought. It didn't matter. He'd extended kindness and safety, neither of which she was in any position to refuse. Especially not while taking care of Daniel.

A crisp breeze scattered dried leaves as Sierra followed Kyle wordlessly up the walkway. The diaper bag was thrown over his broad shoulder and, against the long line of his back, looked tiny. He used his thumbprint to unlock the front door.

Inside, the house was cozy. A leather sectional was arranged in front of a fireplace and television. Blankets and magazines were stacked in baskets underneath the side tables. Through the doorway on the left, a dining room and farm-style kitchen were visible. Photos were scattered about.

A tabby meowed from the top of a cat tree. The tower had a plush hiding hole, multiple levels, and enough dangling toys to keep the busiest feline happy. Sierra blinked. "That's a huge cat tree. I've never seen anything like it."

"That's because I built it. Ms. Whiskers deserves nothing but the best." Kyle held out his hands and the tabby took a flying leap into his arms. Several notches were missing from her ears, but her fur was silky smooth. Ms. Whisker purred, rubbing her head on Kyle's chest, before blinking her multicolored eyes at him in adoration. Kyle stoked her back. "I rescued her from the trash can as a kitten."

Something inside Sierra's heart twisted. If she needed any more proof that Kyle was exactly the kind of man he'd held himself out to be, this was it. And it struck a chord of loneliness inside her. Would she ever find someone to love? Someone as kind and good as Kyle?

No. Romance wasn't possible, and tonight's attack only drove home the importance of keeping to herself. No one deserved to be targeted by her family. Sierra sighed, shifting Daniel's carrier from one arm to the other. The baby had fallen asleep.

"Sorry, I've forgotten my manners." Kyle lowered Ms. Whiskers to the floor and then reached out his hand. "Want me to take Daniel?"

"No, I've got it." She smiled ruefully. "But please don't worry if you hear me in the kitchen later on tonight. Daniel still wakes up every three to four hours for a bottle. I hope that won't be a bother."

"Not at all. Make yourself at home. Let me show you to the guest room so you can put Daniel down and get settled."

She followed him to a bedroom in the rear of the house. It had a four-poster bed and an ensuite bathroom. Kyle set the diaper bag on an overstuffed armchair facing the large window overlooking the property. A reading nook? That's what it looked like. Sierra was tempted to sit, but she was suddenly so exhausted, she feared never getting back up again.

"There are fresh sheets on the bed." Kyle flipped on the bathroom light. "Spare toothbrushes and other travel needs in the cabinet underneath the sink." He eyed her carefully, and the scrutiny caused a heat to rise in her cheeks. "My mom may have some clothes you could borrow—"

"No need. I pack an extra set of clothes in the diaper bag." Sierra gently set Daniel's carrier on the carpet next to the bed. "Babies are prone to spitting up. He's done it at the most inopportune times, like right before going into church. Thank goodness for wrinkle-free slacks. That material can be crumpled into a ball, but still presentable after a quick shake."

She was rambling. An old habit she'd formed as a teenager to avoid difficult or awkward situations. Sierra took a deep breath and forced herself to meet his gaze. "I'll be fine. Thanks."

He nodded. "If there's anything you need, just holler. I'm in the bedroom at the other end of the hall."

Sierra offered him another smile, fully expecting he would leave, but Kyle stood rooted to the spot. They stood there in silence for a moment. She could sense he wanted to say something, but was debating the wisdom of doing so. It sent a jolt of fear through her. Sierra would lie if she had to, as she'd done when asked about the bullet holes, but it wasn't something she wanted to do.

Kyle gestured toward Daniel. "I don't have a crib..."

Her shoulders sagged in relief, even as a wave of tenderness washed over her. It was exceedingly kind of him to think of Daniel's comfort. "That's okay. He prefers to sleep in the carrier. Even when we're at home, he ends up spending the night there most of the time." Sierra made shooing motions with her hands. "Go on, Kyle. I promise to shout if I need anything."

He took the hint and spun on his heel, but then he paused, turning back to catch her eye. "You're safe here, Sierra. Both of you."

A lump filled her throat as emotion threatened to overwhelm her. The caring in his eyes nearly undid her. Before Sierra could find her tongue, Kyle left, gently shutting the door behind him.

She released a breath and sank into the armchair next to the window. The silence enveloped her, broken only by Daniel's soft breathing. She checked her watch. He wouldn't need to eat for another few hours. The smart thing would be to wash her face, brush her teeth, and climb into bed. But Sierra didn't feel like her mind would rest until she had a plan.

First things first, she needed to get as far away from Knoxville as possible. She disappeared once—with her mother and sister—she could do it again. Where had her mother obtained the false birth certificates? Sierra had no idea, but changing her identity would be necessary. Daniel's too. But that was a worry for a later time.

She needed cash. There was plenty in her go-bag stored at the bus station locker, enough for tickets out of town and to establish a new life someplace else. She didn't care where they ended up, as long as it was outside of Texas. Getting to the bus station would be the biggest problem. She sensed Kyle wouldn't drive her there himself. Not without asking a lot of questions she didn't want to answer.

Would he call the police in the morning? It was a genuine possibility. She needed to be gone by daybreak.

With a sinking feeling, Sierra realized she'd have to steal his truck. She'd leave it at the bus station and then call him to say where it was. It was a terrible way to repay his kindness, but her options were limited. The men who'd broken into her house had attempted to kidnap Daniel.

Oliver wanted him. Sierra didn't need to ask why. Her father didn't have any children with Cece, and he'd always wanted an heir. A son was preferred, but a grandson was the next best thing. Daniel's safety had to take precedence.

Sierra quickly got ready for bed, checked to make sure Daniel was comfortable, and then slid between the soft cotton sheets. But sleep eluded her. Every time she closed her eyes, the images from the attack in her home plagued her. She ran through it again and again in slow motion. The hitman could've killed her before she'd even known he was there. But he didn't. Because he wanted something...

Files.

And one question above all wouldn't leave her: What files?

SIX

The next morning, Kyle guzzled a cup of coffee as he crossed the yard to the barn. The sun hadn't broken over the horizon yet, and fog hung low on the ground. Normally, he'd do a five-mile run before seeing to the ranch chores, but this morning, exhaustion seeped into his bones. He'd spent the entire night researching Sierra.

What he found created more questions than answers.

"Morning, cuz." Nathan Hollister slammed the door shut on his pickup truck. He had a takeaway cup in his hand—probably coffee—prepared by his lovely wife, Cassie. They lived on the other side of town. Nathan had his own horse farm, but since Kyle's parents were away, he'd stopped by to lend a helping hand.

His cousin took one look at Kyle's expression and his brows arched. "What's got your underwear in a knot?"

"I ran into some trouble last night and I'm not sure what to do about it." Kyle scowled. "Do you remember Sierra Lyons?"

He gave a rundown of last night's events while they set the horses out to graze and mucked stalls. Ranch hands, housed on the other side of the property, would see to the grazing cattle. White Oak

35

Ranch was over one thousand acres. It took a tremendous amount of time and energy to maintain and manage.

Kyle leaned against the pitchfork. "After we came home last night, I did some digging. Turns out Sierra Lyons isn't her real name."

Nathan's mouth dropped open. "Are you sure?"

"Positive." Kyle had been part of an elite reconnaissance unit in the Army. It was a part of his career he never discussed since the missions were classified, but he was an expert hacker and still occasionally freelanced for companies to shore up their security systems. In this case, he'd used his skills to dig into Sierra's claims. Nathan was one of the few people who knew about Kyle's true capabilities. "And get this. Her entire family was lying about their identities. They have birth certificates, but it didn't take me long to figure out they're excellent forgeries."

"Do you know who Sierra really is?"

"No, but I found it strange Sierra's family packed up and left Knoxville without a word in the middle of the night all those years ago. Like they were running from something. Or someone."

Nathan nodded. "And now she's back with professional hitmen on her tail."

"Yep. Unfortunately, I don't have enough information to piece together what's really going on, and Sierra isn't being forthright. Whatever trouble she's in, I think it started when she was a child." He rubbed his forehead. A headache was brewing along the front of his scalp. "How do I convince her to tell me the truth?"

"I'm not sure that's your job. Seems to me the wisest course of action is to call Chief Garcia. Uncle Rob and Aunt Gerdie are due back from Waco this afternoon. The ranch has a security system, but that's not enough. Those hitmen won't give up. Can you be certain someone from the diner won't remember seeing you and Sierra together last night?"

"No." Frustration built inside Kyle. "But I also can't turn this matter over to the police without knowing the key facts. Sierra specifically said that she couldn't trust law enforcement. They could be bought."

Nathan's nostrils flared. "Chief Garcia would never—"

Kyle shook his head, cutting off his cousin's indigent rebuttal. "No, *he* wouldn't, but the chief can't vouch for every single member of his department. He also needs to follow specific rules, which might require bringing in the state police or the FBI. I can't, in good conscience, do anything to put Sierra and Daniel in danger."

What am I supposed to do here, God?

His cell phone beeped with a warning bell. Kyle tugged it from his pants pocket and scrolled to the security app. Something—or someone—had triggered the camera in front of the house. His muscles stiffened as the feed appeared on his phone.

"What is it?" Nathan asked.

Sierra, carrying Daniel, flew off the porch. The diaper bag was slung over one shoulder, and she cast a quick glance over the other, as if half expecting someone to appear behind her. She ran for Kyle's truck. What was she doing?

The headlights flickered as she unlocked the vehicle. Confusion gave way to anger as Kyle realized the intent of her actions.

He broke into a run. "Sierra's stealing my truck."

The bus terminal was crowded with people. Commuters carrying briefcases and laptop bags maneuvered around families with small children. The place smelled of sweat, old french fries, and gasoline. Sierra hurried to the lockers lining the back wall. She glanced over her shoulder. Since arriving, she couldn't shake the feeling that she was being watched, but no one seemed to pay her any mind. Daniel, fed and with a clean diaper, slept peacefully in the sling attached to her chest.

Quickly, she entered the code for the locker and it clicked open.

She pulled out her go-bag before placing Kyle's truck keys inside. Sunlight caught on the emblem attached to the key ring, and Sierra immediately recognized the Bible verse etched in the metal. She traced the letters with her finger and whispered the words aloud, "Be strong and courageous; do not be frightened and do not be dismayed, for the Lord your God is with you wherever you go."

It was an apt reminder, given the situation she was in. Sierra was grateful for it. Before releasing the key chain, she sent up a silent prayer for Kyle. Once again, although he didn't know it, he'd provided a helping hand.

For the dozenth time, Sierra second-guessed the decision to walk away from his offer of protection. But it would be reckless to accept. Kyle had a family and ranch full of workers to take care of. She wouldn't put anyone else in danger. Once she was in a safe place and could purchase a burner phone, she'd text Kyle explaining how to retrieve the keys.

She slammed the locker shut. Her gaze drifted over the bus terminal. Nothing seemed amiss. She brushed a kiss across the top of Daniel's downy head. "Let's catch our ride out of town, little one."

Juggling the diaper bag, her go-bag, and the car seat wasn't an easy feat, but all of them were necessary. She headed for the counter to purchase bus tickets out of town. A man appeared in her peripheral vision, stepping from a hallway leading to the employee section of the terminal.

Evan, her father's right-hand man.

Before Sierra could react, Evan wrapped an arm around her waist and jabbed something in her side. A gun. The barrel pressed into her kidney and she yelped in response.

"Don't scream or make a scene. If you do, I'll be forced to shoot anyone who comes to your aid." His voice was a low whisper in her ear, but the tone sent chills down her spine. "Do you want the blood of innocent people on your hands?"

She swallowed hard. Evan would follow through on his threat,

Sierra was certain. Her heart beat frantically and thoughts pinged around her mind like a pinball machine. She was a fool. She should've taken Kyle's warning—about her inability to outrun these dangerous men with a baby—more seriously. Trying to do the right thing had put her in this impossible predicament.

Why hadn't she just stolen Kyle's truck and driven it across the country? Because she didn't want to hurt him. He'd treated her with kindness, and outright stealing his vehicle with the intention of never returning it was beyond the limits of even her faulty moral compass.

People hurried past without a second glance. To an outsider, they looked like a couple. Evan stood close, the weapon hidden from view by Sierra's body. His gray suit melded in with the rest of the commuters bustling around them and the gel holding Evan's dark hair in place was shiny under the fluorescent lights. He was pushing late-thirties, but his face remained unlined.

As a child, Sierra had considered him to be the most handsome man she'd ever seen. Uncle Evan, she'd called him. He'd eaten at their dining room table and given her piggy back rides. But nothing could erase the flat look in his eyes. How had she missed it, even as a youngster?

He jabbed the gun deeper into her side. "Start walking to the parking lot."

One protective hand on Daniel, the other still clutching the car seat, Sierra followed Evan's instructions. She was grateful the hitman hadn't shot her on the spot. Buying time was the only answer. She had to figure out a way to break away from him, but his grip was impossibly strong. Her insides trembled. Sierra dragged her feet. "Let me leave Daniel here. He's an innocent baby who has nothing to do with this."

Evan didn't respond. The automatic door swished open and the cool air washed over Sierra's heated cheeks. Her mind raced, desperately seeking a way to slow down the kidnapping. "You want the files."

That caught his attention. Evan glanced at her sharply and a muscle in his jaw twitched. "What do you know about the files?"

Nothing, but if she could use the information to her advantage, then it might provide an opportunity to escape. She slowed her steps even more. "I put them in the locker. Inside."

Evan's expression was cold and deadly. "Don't lie to me, Jacqueline." Her birth name on his lips sent a shudder through her body. "You aren't good at it. The only thing in that locker was your bag. I'm sure the files are in there."

"No, they aren't."

His eyes bore into hers. They were black pits of hatred, and although Sierra was telling the truth, she couldn't stop herself from dropping her gaze. An invisible vise squeezed her chest, making it difficult to breathe.

Evan snorted. Then he forced her to keep walking by jabbing the gun harder into Sierra's side. "It wasn't smart for your sister to dig into things."

This time when Sierra stumbled, it was for real. "Lucy? What does Lucy have to do with this?"

"Enough with the questions." Evan forced her to keep walking by jabbing the gun harder into Sierra's side. "Just do as I say, and everything will be fine."

She didn't believe one word. Evan's vehicle was a short distance away. Sierra recognized it from the diner. She sucked in a breath and clamped down on the panic threatening to overwhelm her. A physical confrontation was her only answer. It was incredibly risky, especially with Daniel strapped to her chest, but once they were inside Evan's car...their chances of escape were slim. Time was running out.

She wrapped her arm around the baby to shield him and tightened her grip on the car seat. The plastic bit into her palm. Her first instinct was to swing the heavy object toward Evan's head, but they were between two cars and her movements were restricted.

"Hey, mister, do you know the route to Alabama?" A loud voice said from the end of the aisle.

Sierra's gaze shot to the innocent man who'd stumbled into a dangerous situation. She smothered a gasp, even as her heart leapt.

Kyle.

His plaid button-down and blue jeans were rumpled and dusty, as if he'd been doing farm work. A worn cowboy hat covered his hair and shielded his eyes from the sun while a pair of thick-framed black glasses gave him a harmless school-boy appearance. As impossible as it seemed, he'd rounded his broad shoulders and folded his spine, which shaved an inch or two from his towering height. One hand clutched a crumpled map. He looked nothing like the strong, capable man she'd met yesterday.

How...? Why...? Her mind couldn't make sense of the situation, but Sierra shoved those questions aside. All that mattered was getting Daniel out of danger.

Kyle completely ignored Sierra and the baby, instead focusing on the man gripping her arm. His lips curved into a disarming smile. "Sorry to bother y'all, but I'm all turned around." A thick Southern drawl flavored his words and he spoke with a slower tempo. "I'm trying to get to Alabama. Do you know the route I take to get to I-10?"

Evan obviously didn't want to draw attention to the fact that he was holding Sierra at gunpoint. He plastered something akin to a pleasant smile on his face. "No, sorry." He pulled Sierra closer and took a step toward Kyle, who was blocking their path to Evan's vehicle. "We're in something of a hurry."

"I'm sure if you just look at the map, you'll be able to tell." Kyle ambled in their direction. "I get so turned around in places like this. It's a lot bigger than my town. I'm from Oklahoma. We've got more cows than people." He laughed at his own joke and took another step forward. "Ever been to Oklahoma, mister? Got the prettiest sunset you'd ever hope to see."

In a flash, Kyle's fist came up and rammed into Evan's face. The force of the blow sent the man slamming into the vehicle behind him. Sierra stumbled and nearly fell as the hitman slid to the ground. She instinctively dropped the carrier to wrap her arms around Daniel to protect him.

A firm hand shot out and grasped her elbow. Kyle's touch was strong enough to stop her from falling, but his grip was still gentle. Sierra didn't have time to utter a word before he dropped his hand from her arm and bent to grab the car seat handle. "Let's go."

She stared at him, barely processing his words. Then her gaze shot to Evan. He was knocked out cold, the gun he'd used to threaten her lying on the pavement beside him. Her go-bag was next to him. She grabbed it. "I need this." Bile threatened to rise up and choke her as a wave of dizziness swirled her vision. Her legs trembled. Sierra feared she might collapse.

Kyle took the bag from her hands and tossed it over his shoulder before grasping her forearm. "Sierra, let's go. There are two more men closing in on our location." He tugged her forward. "Run!"

SEVEN

No one was following them.

Kyle let out the breath he was holding and loosened his grip on the steering wheel. The ranch's work truck wasn't much to look at. It was covered in dust, the fabric on the seats worn, and the front dash faded from sun damage. But the engine purred like Ms. Whiskers as they flew down the freeway. Billboards, fast-food restaurants, and speed limit signs blurred together.

In the passenger seat, Sierra gripped the door handle. Her knuckles were white against the black pleather. Daniel, tucked in his car seat, was nestled between them. It wasn't an ideal location for the baby—the rear seats in the old extended cab were safer—but the base of the carrier was strapped in and secure. A miracle given their narrow escape from the hitmen chasing them. The black-rimmed frames Kyle had used as part of his disguise rattled in the cup holder. Both his parents used reading glasses. They left them all over the house and in every vehicle.

Sierra's gaze was focused on his face, the weight of her stare as physical as a touch. Kyle spared a glance in her direction before checking the rearview mirror again. No sign of the gunmen. "What?"

"Who are you?" Her voice was incredulous.

He snorted. "I was about to ask you the same question."

Sierra arched a brow. Kyle sighed, recognizing the wisdom of playing it straight with her in the hopes she would do the same. "I was a security specialist in the Army. I'm trained in tactics, both offensive and defensive."

"You followed me."

"You stole my truck." He shot her a look and then focused back on the road. He tamped down the anger and frustration layering his voice. "You were also in danger. I wanted to make sure you were safe."

She was quiet for a long moment. "I'm sorry for taking your truck, but I didn't think you would give me a ride to the bus terminal without asking a bunch of questions. I needed my go-bag. And I wanted to put as much distance between myself and those men as possible." Sierra leaned her head back against the headrest and closed her eyes. "It was a foolish decision, but all I want to do is protect Daniel."

Her voice was small and vulnerable. It tugged at every one of Kyle's protective instincts. He steered the truck off the freeway onto a country road. A small picnic area designed for weary travelers sat to the side. All the tables and benches were empty.

Kyle pulled into the alcove, strategically hiding the truck behind some trees from anyone traveling along the freeway, but he maintained a view of any approaching vehicle. He shoved the gearshift into Park. "I think it's time you and I have an honest conversation about what's going on. I'll start. Your name isn't Sierra Lyons."

She inhaled sharply and her eyes popped open. Sierra met Kyle's gaze. "Who told you that?"

"No one. I researched you last night after we came home. I'm a trained hacker. These days, I use my skills to assist companies shoring up their security defenses, but sometimes it's necessary to check into people. Your story didn't add up last night. My first instinct was to call the police, but I don't like making decisions without having all the facts. My priority was keeping you and Daniel safe."

Sierra released a sigh that seemed to drain the last dredges of strength from her muscles. His chest clenched at the heartache etched on her features. Sierra's complexion was pale. Silky strands of hair had wriggled free from the confines of the braid. They floated in soft waves around her exquisite face. One of her hands was placed over Daniel's body. The baby was sleeping, completely unaware of the dangerous situation he'd narrowly escaped. Kyle didn't want to consider what could've happened to Sierra or the baby if he hadn't intercepted them.

"I want to help, Sierra, but I can't protect you and Daniel if I don't know what's going on. Talk to me."

She was quiet for a long moment and then turned to face him. "You're right. My name isn't really Sierra Lyons. It's Jacqueline Patterson. When I was seven, my mother woke me up in the middle of the night. She bundled my sister and I into coats and snuck us out of the house. We've been running from my father ever since."

A cold finger of dread crept down Kyle's back. "Who's your father?"

"Oliver Patterson."

Shock vibrated through him. He wasn't a member of law enforcement, but almost everyone in the United States knew who Oliver Patterson was. The suspected crime lord had recently been on trial for murder. The media had covered every second of the proceedings.

It was hard to believe the beautiful woman sitting in his truck, and the sweet baby next to her, were related to the leader of an organized crime ring. And yet...the explanation fit with everything Kyle knew. The way Sierra and her family had disappeared after junior prom without warning, the recent attacks against her, and the lies she'd told. "How did your father find you?"

"I'm not sure, but I think my sister has something to do with it." Sierra blew out a breath. "Evan said something during the kidnap attempt. He told me Lucy should've stayed out of it. I don't know what he's talking about, but I'm certain about one thing: my sister and brother-in-law were murdered."

Daniel shifted in the car seat and sent up a whimper. Sierra found the pacifier at the end of a string attached to his clothes and wriggled it between his lips. The baby started sucking.

"I want justice for Lucy, but keeping Daniel safe is more important," she continued. "I didn't lie about everything, but there are things I held back. Two men broke into my house last night. They were going to kill me and kidnap Daniel. I think my father wants to raise him as his own. He doesn't have any children with his new wife, and he's always wanted a boy. A grandson is the next best thing."

Kyle's fingers twitched, and he was tempted to ball his hands into fists. He should've hit Evan harder. "I won't allow anyone to put a hand on you or Daniel. Running isn't working, Sierra. My ranch has a top-of-the-line security system. You'll be safe there."

"For how long?" Her voice was hollow. "It's only a matter of time before they find me. And Kyle, my father and his men won't hesitate to kill you or anyone else I'm with. I don't want to put your family at risk."

"For starters, I'm not that easy to kill, and as for my family, let me worry about them." His parents would be horrified if Kyle didn't help Sierra and Daniel. The Stewarts didn't turn away people in need of protection. "We won't sit around and wait for your father to find you. It's time to involve the police. I know Chief Garcia personally. He's a good man and an excellent cop. If I ask him to come to the ranch alone, and then we explain the circumstances, I'm sure he can find a way to launch an investigation without putting your safety at risk."

She hesitated and then nodded. Daniel took that moment to spit out the pacifier and then released a mighty wail. His eyes screwed up in frustration. He balled one tiny hand into a fist and attempted to suck on it but grew frustrated. Sierra checked her watch. "Right on schedule. It's feeding time."

Kyle reached around the back of her seat for the diaper bag and then handed it to her. Sierra dug around for the items necessary to make a bottle. Daniel's sucking and movements became more frantic. His distress only fueled his aunt's. She hurriedly poured water into the bottle, sloshing some over the sides. "I know, sweetie. Just hold on."

Daniel wailed in reply. A tear leaked from one eye. Kyle couldn't stand it anymore. He fumbled with the belt securing the baby to the seat, and it snapped open. He lifted Daniel awkwardly, trying to keep the baby's head from flopping around.

Finally, he managed to tuck Daniel into the corner of his elbow. The baby wrapped his hand around Kyle's finger. His bright blue eyes blinked in surprise, as if he was shocked to be held by someone new. A warmth spread through Kyle's chest, followed by a gut-wrenching heartache. His fiancée, Maisy, had wanted children as much as Kyle. Her death had left a hole in his heart that would never heal.

Sierra shook the bottle to mix the formula. "I see you haven't lost your touch with little ones."

"The Stewart clan is big on my dad's side. I've got dozens of cousins and second-cousins. There are always loads of us at family get-togethers. You pick up a thing or two about babies and kids, even if only in passing." His nose wrinkled. "I'll spare you the time my Aunt Ginny forced me to learn how to change a diaper."

She chuckled. "I wish your Aunt Ginny had been around to teach me." The smile faded from her face. "I got a crash course in parenting when Lucy died. Literally had to watch online videos to teach myself how to make formula and change diapers. It's too bad there aren't any blogs explaining what to do when your life is threatened and you're on the run with an infant."

Sierra reached for Daniel and gracefully tucked the baby into the right position to feed him. He eagerly grasped the bottle. The truck cab was silent except for the sound of the baby's giant gulps. They brought a smile to Kyle's face. "He loves to eat. How can something so small drink so fast?"

"I have no idea." Sierra shook her head. "Sometimes it's a challenge to wrestle the bottle out of his mouth so I can burp him. The pediatrician said he's in the 90% for his weight and height." She smiled down at Daniel. "You're a growing boy, aren't you? Getting bigger and stronger every day."

Her voice was tender, her expression pure love. It touched something deep inside Kyle, a dormant part of his heart that he'd thought was long dead and buried. He needed to be careful here. Keeping Sierra and Daniel safe was one thing. Letting them wriggle past his defenses was another. Maisy had been the greatest love of his life, and losing her had crippled him. He couldn't go through anything like that again.

Turning his attention back to the matter at hand, Kyle considered their options. Involving Chief Garcia was the first step. The next would be uncovering how Oliver had found Sierra. "Can you think of any way Lucy may have tipped off your father to your whereabouts? Could she have contacted him?"

"No. Lucy wouldn't have done that." Sierra frowned. "The way Evan said it...almost like my sister was investigating something..." Her eyes widened. "The letter."

"What letter?"

"Last night, I received a call from my sister's probate attorney. Lucy had written a letter for me and requested it be delivered with her will, but it was misfiled. The attorney just found it. Initially, I thought it was instructions for how to raise Daniel, but now that I think about it, why didn't she write a letter to her husband? Lucy had no way of knowing he would die in the same accident as she did." Sierra's words came out hurriedly, as if her thoughts were racing. "Whatever she was involved in, Lucy must've known it was risky. She wrote that letter to warn me."

"Where's the attorney's office?"

She popped the bottle out of Daniel's mouth and shifted the baby to her shoulder before gently patting his back. "In Austin."

Taking Sierra and Daniel there would be too dangerous. "Call him and say that Nathan Hollister will pick up the letter. My cousin can meet us back at the ranch." Kyle reached for his cell phone but paused when Sierra's hand landed on his forearm. He glanced up. His heart stuttered at the vulnerability etched across her beautiful features.

Sky blue. That was the color of her eyes. A stunning shade reserved for a cloudless spring day in Texas. He'd never met anyone else with eyes like Sierra's. Something about them reached inside his heart and pounded at the barriers he'd placed to protect himself from heartache and loss.

"I have to ask." She tilted her head, the braid dropping over her left shoulder, shimmering in the sunlight like a raven's wing. "Why are you helping me, Kyle? It would be safer—for you and your family —if you just walked away."

It would be, but Kyle had never taken the easy road, and he wasn't about to start now. His mouth quirked. "I don't wear the military uniform anymore, but that doesn't change who I am or erase the vows I took. Protecting the innocent is what I've been trained to do."

Although he knew better, Kyle couldn't resist placing a hand over hers. Sierra's skin was soft under his palm and decidedly feminine, but there was strength in her grip as she wrapped her fingers around his.

Kyle met her gaze, determination fueling his words. "You can count on me to see this through. I'll keep you and Daniel safe. I promise."

EIGHT

Three hours later, Sierra sat on the couch in Kyle's house. His parents had returned from their trip to Waco and were currently in the kitchen babysitting Daniel. The older couple were as lovely as Sierra remembered. The low murmur of voices filtered from the kitchen as they spoke with Nathan. About her? Most likely. Kyle had explained the situation to his cousin but hadn't had time to fill his parents in before law enforcement arrived.

Police Chief Sam Garcia perched on the recliner. His dark hair was more gray than brown and the lines bracketing his mouth spoke of long hours at a demanding job. He scanned the letter Lucy had hastily scrawled a day before her death.

I've discovered something that could take down Oliver and his entire organization. I'm sorry, sis, but I have to take the risk. For Daniel. If you're reading this, then something went terribly wrong and you're in danger. Contact Jeff Lewis. He can help you.

Seeing her sister's handwriting had been like a gut punch. A mixture of emotions swirled inside Sierra's chest, each fighting for the chance to have its moment. Pain, grief, anger, and betrayal. How could Lucy have kept this from her? They'd been more than sisters. They'd been best friends.

Secrets and lies. Sierra was so tired of both.

The chief frowned. "Any idea who this guy Jeff Lewis is?"

"None, but you see there's a phone number at the bottom of the letter." Sierra pointed to it. "I called it. Jeff answered, but he refused to identify himself other than to say he was Lucy's friend. We have a meeting set up for four o'clock this afternoon at a coffee shop in town."

"Without knowing who this guy is?" The chief's bushy eyebrows rose. "Do you think that's wise?"

"No, but I don't think we have much choice. Jeff seemed as nervous as I was about the meeting. Whatever he knows, it's important, and I don't want to miss the opportunity to find out exactly what my sister was investigating."

"I tried tracing the phone number," Kyle said. The handsome veteran was standing with his arms crossed next to the fireplace. Ms. Whiskers lay on the mantel behind him, napping. "It's a burner phone."

"That makes me even more nervous." Chief Garcia tapped Lucy's letter against his fingers. "You don't have any idea what Lucy may have uncovered, Sierra?"

"Not a clue. My sister worked as an accountant for a large firm. It's possible she stumbled across something through her job." She shrugged. "But that's just a guess."

He nodded. "I'll have officers drive past the coffee shop before and during the meeting. It's unlikely the hitmen will show up there, but better to be safe than sorry. I'll also have your car towed to the evidence shed and processed." Chief Garcia set Lucy's note down on the coffee table. "However, I'll keep your current contact information off the reports. The only person you'll deal with is me for the moment. No one else in law enforcement needs to know where you are."

Relief rippled through Sierra. "Thank you, sir."

The chief rose from the recliner. He tucked his notebook and pen into the pocket of his shirt before pegging Sierra with a stern look. "I'm not ignorant to the rumors about Oliver Patterson and his ability to buy his way out of trouble. Evidence vanishes, witnesses refuse to testify or disappear, and many of his suspected crimes remain unsolved. While I can appreciate your fears about relying on law enforcement, let me assure you that keeping information from me only puts you in more danger. I expect to be kept informed about what Jeff Lewis has to say this afternoon, as well as anything you uncover on your own."

Sierra nodded. Kyle had been right to contact Chief Garcia. The lawman had been thorough and professional. His promise to keep Sierra's identity a secret was for her benefit alone, and she believed the chief would do everything in his power to find and lock up the thugs attacking her. She rose and shook his hand. "You have my word."

He nodded his appreciation and then shook Kyle's hand. "I'd best say my regards to your parents before heading out."

The group went into the kitchen. Kyle's mother, Gerdie, was cooing over Daniel. Her silver hair was cut into a fashionable bob that suited the angles of her face, and she dressed casually in jeans and a lightweight sweater. Kindhearted, with an easy smile, Gerdie was an effortless hostess. She'd instantly made Sierra feel at home.

Rob Stewart rose from his place at the kitchen table to shake the chief's hand. Kyle's father was lean and muscular from decades of ranch work. The shape of his strong nose and the line of his jaw were mirrored in his only son. Nathan was nowhere to be seen.

The three men began conversing about the weather. Sierra joined Gerdie by the window. The older woman immediately offered her a wide smile. "Oh, please don't take him from me yet. It's been a long time since I held such a tiny baby." She jutted her chin toward the kitchen island. "There's fresh iced tea, if you're interested. I hope you like it extra sweet." Gerdie winked. "That's the only way I know how to make it."

"I wouldn't have it any other way." Sierra poured herself a glass and took a long sip. The cool liquid was the perfect blend of lemony tang and crisp sweetness. "That's delicious." She joined Kyle's mom on the window seat. The cushion was firm and the view beyond the glass breathtaking. Horses grazed peacefully in a pasture dotted with wildflowers. "Where's Nathan?"

"He's outside, making a round of the property." Gerdie's smile faltered. "He told us what's been going on. Hon, I can't imagine how difficult this has been. I'm so glad you and Daniel are here. I want you to know that you're welcome for as long as it takes to get to the bottom of things."

Unexpected tears flooded Sierra's eyes. She rapidly blinked them back. "Thank you, Mrs. Stewart. That means more to me than you can know."

The older woman patted her cheek. "Call me Gerdie."

Daniel whimpered. Gerdie swayed him gently, fussing with his blanket and then offering him the pacifier. "Babies are such a blessing. Rob and I both love children, but we found each other late in life. I was nearing forty when Kyle was born. The pregnancy was touch-and-go there for a while, but he and I came out okay." She brushed a finger across Daniel's cheek. "Unfortunately, the doctors told me it would be too dangerous to have more children."

"I'm sorry."

She waved off the apology. "It was a long time ago." She flashed Sierra a smile. "But it means I may fight you for middle-of-the-night feedings and cuddle sessions."

Sierra laughed. "I'm happy to have the help. Although I will warn you, Daniel's prone to colic. There have been more than a few rough nights."

"No one could be worse than my Kyle. I wore a path in the wood floor rocking him to sleep every night. Leave Daniel to me. I'm an old pro."

Rob called out her name, and Gerdie excused herself to speak to her husband and Chief Garcia. Both men instantly melted at the sight of Daniel. It seemed no one in the Stewart house was immune to her nephew's charms, something that brought Sierra a lot of comfort. The little boy had lost his mother and his father. Nothing could make up for that, but extra love and kisses didn't hurt either.

Kyle poured his own glass of ice tea and then sat down next to her on the window seat. He crossed his long legs at the ankle and leaned against the frame. "I hope you realize my mother is going to keep Daniel to herself until it's time for you to leave."

"I'm aware. Although, I think that's a bigger problem for you than it is for me. She's going to have grandbaby fever."

He snorted. "Nathan's the married one. I'll send my mom his way."

Something in the tone of his voice caught her attention. Sierra tilted her head. "Aren't you interested in getting married?"

"No."

She found his answer perplexing. It was none of her business, but curiosity got the better of her. "Any particular reason why?"

Ms. Whiskers wandered past, threading herself through the opening between Kyle's legs and the back of the window seat. He picked the cat up and placed her in his lap. She immediately started purring. Sierra reached out and brushed a hand across the tabby's head. Her fur was silky smooth.

Kyle sighed. "My fiancée died. Two years ago, during her last deployment."

Sierra's hand stilled on Ms. Whisker's head. The pain in his voice broke her heart. "Oh, Kyle, I'm so sorry." Heat infused her cheeks as embarrassment took hold. "I shouldn't have joked about your mom having grandbaby fever. I didn't know—"

"There was no way for you to. Don't apologize." He was quiet for a long moment. "Maisy was a medic. She flew rescue missions, picking up wounded soldiers in some of the most dangerous places in the world. We met on base through some mutual friends. Dated for two years. The day I asked her to marry me was the best day of my life." He swallowed hard. "Her Helo was shot down one month later. Everyone on board died. I was on my own deployment when I got word. It was...devastating."

Devastating was a good word for it. Sierra was intimately familiar with grief and how a sudden loss could shake you to the core. It touched her that Kyle shared his loss with her. She had the sense it wasn't something he spoke about often. "It sounds like Maisy was a wonderful woman."

"She was. After she died, I couldn't imagine myself married to someone else." Kyle set Ms. Whiskers down on the floor and then swiped at his jeans to rid them of the lingering cat hair. "My mom is going to have to make do with a cat for a grandbaby."

Sierra laughed, but a glance at the clock on the wall brought reality crashing back down on her shoulders. It was nearly time for their meeting with Jeff. She brought her thumb to her mouth and chewed on the nail. "Do you think it's safe to leave Daniel on the ranch while we go into town?"

"Absolutely. He'll be well protected. I've called in reinforcements."

She dropped her hand. "Reinforcements?"

"Yep. Remember the guys I told you about at the diner? The veterans I have dinner with every Wednesday?" He waited for her to nod before continuing, "We're close. Like brothers. They volunteered to help. Daniel couldn't have a set of better men protecting him. I'd stake my life on it." His cell phone beeped and Kyle glanced at the screen. His face broke out in a grin. "They're here now, in fact. Come outside with me and I'll introduce you."

Sierra followed him onto the front porch. Freshly cut grass and roses scented the air, and clouds dotted the sky overhead. Several vehicles caravanned up the driveway. One truck was Kyle's, retrieved from the bus station by his friends.

Kyle jogged down the steps to greet the men. Handshakes and brotherly hugs were exchanged. A German shepherd joined the melee, barking with excitement. A scar slashed across his fur on the right-hand side. One of the men gave an order and the dog instantly quieted, coming to heel.

Kyle turned to her. "Sierra, I'd like you to meet my friends." He pointed to the dark-haired man with the dog. "This is Jason Gonzales and his dog, Connor. Both were with the Marines. The ugly redhead over there is Tucker Colburn, former Army Ranger."

"Hey, who are you calling ugly?" Tucker scowled at Kyle good-naturedly. "Have you looked in a mirror?"

Kyle ignored his friend and continued with the introductions, pointing to a tall blond dressed in cargo pants. He was leaning against Kyle's truck. "That's Logan Keller. He's not good for much. Former medic."

Logan scowled, tossing the truck keys to Kyle who caught them in one hand. "I dare you to say that the next time you get shot, Stewart."

"It's my hope no one will be shot," Sierra said. Her insides turned at the very thought. She was deeply touched that Kyle had arranged for a team to protect Daniel. All joking aside, this group of men appeared capable and tough. There was also a warmth and cama-raderie that couldn't be faked.

Gerdie appeared on the porch. "There are my boys. Get your-selves into the kitchen. There's sandwiches and ice tea for the lot of you."

A stampede proceeded to the kitchen. Nathan popped around the corner of the house and joined the group heading inside. Sierra shook her head in amazement. "I shudder to think how fast that group must go through a plate of sandwiches."

Kyle chuckled. "Mom's used to it." His smile faded. "Jason, Tucker, and Logan will stay here to guard Daniel and my parents.

Nathan and another friend of ours, Walker, are going to keep an eye on the coffee shop. Walker's already there. Nathan will follow us in his truck. We won't see him, but trust me, he'll be there."

As if he heard Kyle speaking about him, Nathan reappeared on the porch. He had a sandwich in each hand. He ambled down the steps and joined them on the driveway. He gallantly offered a hoagie to Sierra, but she shook her head. "No, thank you."

"What a relief." Nathan grinned. "I hoped that's what you would say."

Kyle shoved his cousin good-naturedly. "Keep eating like that and you won't be able to keep up during PT."

"I can run circles around you, cuz. Don't worry about me." His expression turned serious, and he focused on Sierra. "The guys will make rounds on the property to ensure no one gets close to the house. I've explained the seriousness of the situation. All of them understand the enemy we're up against. No one will underestimate Oliver's thugs."

Sierra took a deep breath, letting her worries about Daniel's immediate safety ease from her mind. He was in excellent hands. It allowed her to focus on the upcoming meeting with Jeff. She prayed he could provide answers. And that whatever Lucy had uncovered would put Oliver behind bars forever.

Kyle pulled his keys from his pocket. "Ready to go?"

Danger lurked beyond the ranch fence. Sierra knew it, but she also had Kyle by her side. He'd proven to be a fierce protector. It was time to finish what her sister had started. Sierra took a deep breath and squared her shoulders. "Let's do this."

NINE

The center of Knoxville was bustling with activity. Families with children gathered in the town square and shoppers strolled the tree-lined streets. Kyle drove past the church his family attended and pulled into a parking space across from the Roasted Bean. The awning was a cheery yellow. Signage outside proclaimed a free cookie with every purchase of a coffee.

Kyle strolled around the vehicle to open the passenger side door. The space between his shoulder blades prickled, but he resisted swiveling his head to locate the source. He didn't want to draw attention to Sierra's secret protection detail. Walker Montgomery, his friend, was a former Navy SEAL. And Nathan had been a Green Beret. Both men were highly trained, and Kyle trusted them to have his back.

He opened the truck door. Sierra smiled warmly, and his heart skipped a beat. The woman was breathtakingly beautiful. Her sweetness with Daniel, along with her strength and bravery, were an enticing combination, but Kyle refused to allow his feelings to develop beyond friendship. His heart still belonged to Maisy. It always would. This annoying attraction humming between him and

Sierra was just a remnant of their high school romance. It was a distraction Kyle needed to shake.

"I forgot how pretty the town is." Sierra glanced up and down the street, her gaze lingering on the ice cream shop at the corner. It'd been a favorite hangout of theirs. "Please tell me Paulson's still sells root beer floats."

She was making small talk, probably to settle her nerves. Kyle couldn't blame her. "Paulson's still makes root beer floats, although they've added several new ice cream flavors to the menu. A chocoholic like you may have a hard time deciding which one to pick."

A police car drove by. The officer inside met Kyle's gaze and nodded once before continuing on down the road and hanging a right. Chief Garcia was doing his best to keep them safe. Another layer of protection for Sierra. Kyle prayed it would be enough. Jeff Lewis, the man they were meeting, was an unknown element. It was worrisome.

The bell over the door of the coffee shop jangled when Kyle held it open for Sierra. The scents of vanilla, coffee, and chocolate mingled together in a pleasing aroma. His gaze scanned the interior. An elderly couple sat in the rear, sharing a huge slice of cake. Another woman sat next to the window reading a magazine, and several teenagers were chatting in the booths along the far wall. Nothing out of the ordinary.

Sierra's jaw clenched. "He isn't here."

"It doesn't mean he won't show. We're early." Kyle placed a hand on the small of her back, steering her toward the counter. "Let's get some coffee and a cookie while we wait."

They placed an order and then took seats next to the large front window. Kyle angled his chair so he had full view of the interior of the coffee shop along with most of the street. Another police cruiser drove by. Nathan was sitting on a bench under an oak tree eating a pretzel. Walker was nowhere to be seen.

Sierra wrapped her hand around the porcelain coffee mug. "I've

LYNN SHANNON

been meaning to thank you, Kyle. For everything." Her lips lifted at
the corners. "You practically rallied an army to protect Daniel. As
nerve-wracking as this is, I feel much better knowing he's safe."

"You don't need to thank me." He pushed a double chocolate
chip cookie in her direction. "We're friends, Sierra. I know it's been a
long time since high school, but..." Kyle shrugged. "We always had a
connection."

It was the truth. Kyle had friends and was well-liked, but there
weren't many people he shared his deep emotion with. Sierra had
been someone he could freely talk to. Being with her felt natural.
Time and distance hadn't changed that, evidenced by their conversation in the kitchen about Maisy. Kyle couldn't remember the last time
he'd discussed his fiancée's death with anyone. Yet somehow he'd
known Sierra would understand.

She broke off a piece of the cookie. "Distract me. Tell me more
about your friends. How did you guys all meet if you're from
different branches of the military?"

"We met after being discharged. Nathan and Jason were room-
mates at the veterans hospital, so when I started visiting my cousin,
we all became friends. The group grew over time as we met more
guys in the area who were transitioning from military to civilian life."
Kyle took a sip of his coffee. "We formed something of a support
group for each other. There are some things only someone else from
the military can understand."

"I get that." Sierra's expression grew distant. "It was like that for
me and Lucy. We couldn't tell anyone who we really were. My sister
was the only person I could truly be myself around."

For the first time, Kyle realized the extent of Sierra's loss. And her
loneliness. "That must've been hard to handle, especially as a kid."

"It was. To be honest, I haven't handled it well as an adult either.
It's difficult to make deep friendships when you can't be honest.
Falling in love was out of the question too. I didn't want to lie to my
husband, but I couldn't tell him the truth either."

60

"Lucy managed it. She got married, had a baby."

Sierra sighed, setting down the broken cookie piece without eating it. "My sister never fully appreciated how tenuous our situation was. She was so little when we escaped from my father. She didn't have any memories of him." Her jaw hardened. "I do."

Kyle's stomach twisted. "Did he hurt you?"

"Not physically, but my father always frightened me. There was something about him that was...unsettling." She was quiet for a long moment. "When I was five, my mother got a dog for me. A Labrador. Shelly and I were inseparable, but she despised my father and avoided him. One night, Oliver came home while we were playing. He went to pet Shelly and she bit him. As an adult, I can see now that she was protecting me..."

"But your father didn't like it."

Her fingers gripped the mug, turning white with the effort. "He shot her. In front of me."

Horror snaked through Kyle. He couldn't fathom how traumatic that experience must've been. Family had always been his safe place. He leaned closer. "I'm so sorry. No one should have to go through that."

"No, they shouldn't." She took a deep breath and let it out slowly. "Afterward, Oliver told me one thing: Never betray the family. My mother later said that's when she knew it was time to leave him. Their marriage wasn't a happy one, but she'd taken her wedding vows seriously and tried to make things work. After the shooting, she began researching my father and discovered who he truly was."

"She didn't know before?"

"Mom may have suspected, but there wasn't a lot of information about Oliver back then. Most of it was rumors. And he kept my mother isolated from everyone except those he deemed acceptable. No one would tell her the truth."

Kyle recognized the pattern of control and abuse. Jason's wife, Addison, was an attorney who worked with women escaping domestic violence. She'd educated them about how insidious a crime it could be. He applauded Sierra's mom for rescuing her daughters from Oliver. It couldn't have been easy.

He ran his thumb over Sierra's knuckle, purposefully ignoring how soft her skin was. "Your mom sounds like a very brave woman."

"She was." Sierra squeezed his hand. "I miss her terribly. Lucy too. Daniel is all I have left in the world, and I'll do whatever's necessary to protect him."

"You won't have to do it by yourself. You're not alone in this, Sierra."

He'd meant the words to be reassuring, but then she met his gaze, and something sparked between them. A warning bell flared in Kyle's brain followed by an avalanche of guilt. Sierra's eyes widened as if whatever he was fighting, she was feeling it too. He pulled his hand away under the guise of picking up his coffee mug. Maisy's face flashed in his mind's eye. They hadn't shared wedding vows, but the day they got engaged, he'd made her a promise all the same.

Kyle cleared his throat, desperate to find a way back to solid friendship ground with Sierra. "My family and I will do everything we can to help you."

"I know that, Kyle, and I'm grateful." Sierra fiddled with the cross necklace at her throat. She worried her bottom lip with her teeth before her expression hardened. "I've spent far too long with secrets and lies. I don't want anymore."

She straightened her shoulders, dropped the cross, and turned to face him. "I have to be truthful with you. There's something between us. More than friendship. It's always been there, even when we were teenagers, and long before we shared our first kiss. But it can't go anywhere. My life is in complete chaos, and there's no guarantee I won't end up on the run." Sierra scanned his expression. "And I sense that your heart still belongs to Maisy."

Something akin to relief weakened his muscles. "It does."

She nodded. "Okay then. We understand each other." Sierra

smiled, leaning back in her chair. "I can't tell you how fantastic that feels."

"To clear the air?"

"To be honest."

Before Kyle could respond, a flash of color beyond the window pane caught his attention. A man in a dark green ball cap was strolling down the sidewalk. Nothing about him was noticeable. He was average height and weight, moving at a steady pace behind a family with a pack of kids, but there was the faint outline of a concealed handgun underneath his lightweight jacket. The weapon itself wasn't unusual. It was Texas, after all. But then the man glanced over his shoulder before crossing the road toward the coffee shop. In that moment, Kyle understood what had caught his attention.

The man carried himself as if he was on guard.

"Looks like Jeff is here." Kyle jutted his chin toward the door. "Recognize him?"

The bells over the door of the coffee shop jangled as the man entered. Sierra turned in her chair and then whispered, "Not at all."

Tension coiled in Kyle's stomach. Jeff's gaze widened when he caught sight of Sierra, and he beelined straight for her. Kyle rose from his chair, placing himself in a protective position. Just in case. They still didn't know who they were dealing with.

"Sierra, it is you." Relief flooded Jeff's expression. "I'm sorry for being so cryptic on the phone, but I couldn't be sure of your identity. I'm glad you called."

Sierra frowned. "I'm sorry, have we met before?"

"Not in person, but your sister talked about you all the time." For the first time, Jeff seemed to register that she didn't know who he was. He glanced at Kyle and then focused back on Sierra. He sighed. "Lucy didn't tell you a thing, did she?"

"No."

Jeff seemed dumbfounded. Kyle arched his brows. "It might help if you explain who you are and how you know Lucy."

The remark seemed to snap some sense into the other man. Jeff reached into his jacket pocket and pulled out a black wallet. He opened it, revealing official identification and a badge. "I'm an agent with the FBI, and Lucy was my informant."

TEN

Shock reverberated through Sierra, catching her off guard in its intensity. She'd known her sister was investigating their father based on the contents of her letter, but actually hearing the words spoken out loud was a different matter altogether. Her baby sister had been an informant for the FBI?

Oh, Lucy. Why didn't you tell me?

Sierra sank into her chair. The coffee she'd drank swirled in her gut like battery acid, threatening to make her sick. "I think you're going to need to start at the beginning, Agent Lewis."

Jeff hesitated, his gaze shooting toward Kyle. "It may be better if we speak in private—"

"There's no need." Sierra briefly explained everything she'd been through over the last several days, starting with the attack in her house and ending with the phone call to Jeff. The agent grew pale when she described how close Oliver's thugs had come to kidnapping Daniel.

Kyle reclaimed his seat, scooting his chair closer to her. His strong presence was protective and comforting. Their conversation from earlier had drawn a boundary line around their friendship. It enabled

Sierra to lean on him without fretting over how Kyle might interpret her actions. The last thing she needed was romance. Or any more confusion. Her life was spiraling out of control with no end in sight.

Jeff grabbed a chair from an empty table nearby and sat. His expression was sympathetic. "First, allow me to offer my belated condolences on your sister's death. Lucy and I hung in the same circle of people in college. That's how we first met and became friends. I always liked her."

Another surprise. Sierra had never heard her sister mention Jeff before, but maybe they hadn't been close. Or perhaps she didn't know Lucy as well as she thought. It was a heartbreaking concept to consider.

"Let me also say that I'm aware of your real identity, Sierra." Jeff kept his voice pitched low so no one else in the coffee shop could hear their conversation. "Lucy told me everything several weeks ago. I've kept the information limited to myself and my boss, so I don't believe that's how Oliver found you, but I thought you should be aware of what I know."

No wonder Lucy hadn't mentioned a word of this to Sierra. She would've been livid to learn her sister had divulged their true identities to anyone. Most members of law enforcement were honest people trying to do their best, but there were those among their ranks who would betray the vows they'd taken for the right price. Or worse, if their families were threatened. Oliver was capable of using both means to get what he wanted.

At this point, it didn't matter how her father found them. Sierra's job was to protect Daniel, and the best way to do that was by focusing on what Lucy had uncovered. "My sister's letter mentioned she was investigating something concerning Oliver. What was it?"

Jeff leaned back in his chair. "How much do you know about Blackstorm's illegal activities?"

"Only what's in the news or online. It's my understanding Blackstorm traffics in weapons, drugs, and people. They launder their money through legitimate businesses such as dry cleaners and restaurants." Like Lucy, Sierra was an accountant. She was well-versed in ways organized crime hid their criminal activity. "Did Lucy find something while working for her accounting firm?"

Jeff nodded. "She was convinced one of her clients was involved with Blackstorm. It's not common knowledge, but Oliver has been expanding his operation for quite some time. He's been opening businesses in several states, including Texas. He also recently bought a house in Austin."

The world tilted and swirled. Her father was living within 50 miles of her. Sierra's breathing quickened as terror sank into her. She battled it back. "Which client did Lucy suspect was involved with Blackstorm?"

"I don't know." Jeff blew out a breath. Frustration thinned the line of his mouth. "Lucy refused to tell me anything until she was certain. A week later, she called to say she'd found enough proof to bring down the entire organization. We agreed to meet the next day, but Lucy died before we could."

Rage unlike anything Sierra had ever experienced jolted through her. She glared at Jeff. "So when Lucy died, you didn't think to contact me and let me know what she was involved in?"

He had the decency to look sheepish. "Honestly, no. The investigation into her accident proved it was a combination of bad weather and shoddy brakes."

She curled her fingers into fists. "Except I explained to the investigators that my brother-in-law had the brakes serviced two months ago." Her voice shook with emotion. "You knew my sister was investigating a connection to Blackstone, and within hours of contacting you to say she'd found enough evidence to take the entire organization down, she's killed. You thought that was a coincidence? I don't know what they've taught you in the FBI, Agent Lewis, but even I know that's suspicious. I—"

Sierra cut herself off before she uttered the ugly words hovering on her tongue. She closed her eyes, fighting for control. The depths of her anger scared her. It always had. Her mother had pushed her into self-defense courses, but Sierra had resisted them, unwilling to risk unleashing her temper.

The recent attacks had demolished her self-restraint. Maybe Sierra should blame Lucy, but she didn't. Her sister had stumbled into something dangerous and tried to take the right steps to safeguard herself and her family. Her death should've been a giant red flag to the FBI. Sierra and Daniel should've been protected.

Kyle's hand closed around her right fist. His touch grounded her, and she took a deep breath to calm her runaway emotions.

"For what it's worth," Kyle growled. "I agree with Sierra. You left her and Daniel out on their own. It's a miracle they weren't killed."

It was a miracle. God—and Kyle—had saved them. Sierra unfisted her hand and interlocked her fingers with Kyle's, accepting the support he offered so freely. It didn't come easily to her. She'd been on her own for a long time, but that hadn't served her well. It took these attacks to make her realize what God had been whispering to her heart for a long time. She needed to let people in.

Jeff scrubbed a hand over his face. "Hold on, guys. Hindsight is always 20/20. Yes, I should've dug deeper into Lucy's death, but I read the reports. Everything seemed on the up and up. Besides, I couldn't be sure Lucy had found anything of value. There was no reason to believe anyone had murdered her."

Sierra raised a brow. "And now?"

"Now, the investigation into her death will be reopened. But I can't promise it'll help. Assuming Oliver figured out what your sister uncovered, he didn't run her off the road himself."

No. Her father would've sent his hitmen, just as he'd done with Sierra.

A pained look crossed Jeff's face. "I'm sorry. I should've contacted you immediately after Lucy's death, but I truly didn't believe her car accident was suspicious. I was wrong."

She studied the agent sitting across from her. His apology rang with sincerity, but was it an act? Could he be trusted? She wasn't sure. His actions after Lucy's death didn't inspire confidence, but he was right in hindsight being 20/20. Mistakes happened, even grave ones.

Once again, Sierra reminded herself of what was important. Protecting Daniel. Her father's arrest and conviction was the best way to accomplish that, which meant Sierra needed the FBI's help. "If I can figure out what Lucy uncovered about Blackstorm, then we can use it to stop Oliver, right?"

Jeff froze and then nodded. "How would you do that?"

"I have access to Lucy's work files via the cloud. She was an independent contractor for the accounting firm, so she kept copies of everything." It was a habit her sister had formed early in her career. Sierra was sure whatever Lucy had found would be saved in those files. "It'll take some time to go through them all—"

"You don't need to do that. If you have legal access to the files, then you can send them directly to me. I'll have our accountants go through them." Jeff pulled out his cell phone. "Hold on, let me call my boss. I want to make sure we dot every *i* and cross every *t*. I don't want to take Oliver down only to have the evidence thrown out on a technicality."

He hit a button on his phone and rose from the table before walking a short distance away. The murmur of his voice drifted across the coffee shop, but not the actual words. Kyle watched him with a scowl on his face. "I'm not sure it was a good idea to tell him you have access to Lucy's work files."

"I agree, but there aren't many options. Besides, I don't plan to hand over any of the files until I've gone through them. Whatever Agent Lewis knows, I want to know too." She mulled over the possibilities in her mind. "We can also give a copy of the files to Chief Garcia. I'm sure he has contacts in the FBI."

Kyle nodded. "Good thinking."

His phone vibrated. Kyle released Sierra's hand to remove it from his pocket. He frowned. "It's Walker."

Sierra hadn't met Kyle's friend yet, but she recognized the name. Walker was somewhere nearby with Nathan, keeping watch over the coffee shop. Her muscles tightened and her gaze shot to the sidewalk beyond the window pane. Traffic on Main Street was building now that it was nearing six o'clock, but nothing seemed out of the ordinary.

Kyle answered. Walker's voice poured from the phone speaker, loud enough for Sierra to overhear.

"Sniper! Roof, one o'clock."

Sierra's heart jumped into her throat as Kyle wrapped an arm around her waist. Glass shattered as he pulled her to the floor. A bullet thumped into Sierra's chair where she'd been sitting only a breath earlier. Screams from the other patrons in the coffee shop erupted.

"Get down!" Kyle ordered. He grabbed the table with one hand and yanked it down in front of Sierra for protection. There was nowhere else for them to hide.

More glass shattered. Sierra bit back a scream as Kyle covered her body with his. Bullets whizzed around them, thumping into the table and the wall. Her chest squeezed tight as fear strangled her. For herself. For Kyle. For the innocent people around them. Sierra was helpless to make it stop.

There was nothing she could do but hold on to Kyle.

And pray.

ELEVEN

Hours later, Kyle prowled the length of his office on the ranch. Frustration and anger fueled his steps. No one had been injured in the coffee shop shooting, by the grace of God, but the attacks against Sierra were increasing in their intensity.

"The sniper escaped in a red Chevy pickup." Walker's tone filled with disgust. He tossed his cowboy hat on the desk before dropping onto the couch. His bulky frame took up more than one cushion. The man was built like a tank but surprisingly quick on his feet. He'd chased the sniper from the rooftop of the hairdresser to the parking lot behind the hardware store. "I wasn't close enough to get the license plate. Chief Garcia is going to pull the surveillance cameras of the grocery store and the gas station at the corner. Maybe we'll get a lead from that."

Kyle wasn't hopeful. "The truck is probably stolen. These men are professionals." He opened the desk and pulled out several photographs he'd found online. "This is Evan Rodriguez and George Sampson. Both are rumored to have worked for Oliver for years. They've each been arrested for various things—assault, domestic battery, even murder—but none of the charges have stuck. Neither has spent a night in prison. They're careful. And deadly."

Walker frowned. "Today's shooting was an act of desperation. I mean...yes, the sniper escaped. But the attempt to kill Sierra wasn't subtle. Most professional hitmen are far more cautious."

"They want Sierra dead at any cost." Kyle quickly ran through what he'd learned from Agent Lewis. "If Lucy did uncover enough evidence to shut down Blackstorm, then Oliver won't risk anyone finding it. He'll do everything he can to silence Sierra."

"Murdering Sierra isn't his only objective." Jason reached down to stroke Connor's head. The German shepherd leaned into the touch. "While you were at the coffee shop, several individuals attempted to breach the ranch security system."

Kyle stiffened. "What? Why didn't you say something earlier—"

"You had your hands full." Jason's jaw tightened. The long scar along his cheek flexed. "I handled it."

He'd offended his friend. Jason was right to be irritated. He was a trained solider who'd faced down some of the worst terrorists in the world. He didn't deserve to be snapped at, especially since Jason would give his life to protect Daniel, no questions asked.

Kyle took a deep breath to temper his emotions. "Of course you handled it. Sorry for the attitude. It's been a long day. What happened?"

The anger in Jason's expression gave way to understanding. He nodded in silent acknowledgment of the apology. "The security system alerted us to a breach on the west end of the ranch. Logan and I responded, but the intruders were gone by the time we arrived." He patted his dog's head. "Connor tracked them through the woods to the road. Chances are, they spotted the cameras along the fence line and reconsidered their approach. I've looked at the footage. It was two men, dressed in black clothing. They aren't identifiable."

Kyle whipped out his phone and pulled up the footage himself. He watched the intruders approach the fence line, notice the cameras, and then retreat. Their vehicle was a dark-colored SUV with missing plates. Kyle watched the incident twice more. "One of these men is Evan Rodriguez, I'm sure of it. He has a distinctive swagger to his gait."

Walker crossed his arms over his chest. "They're after Daniel."

Kyle nodded. "They've been trying to kidnap him since the initial attack at Sierra's house. According to her, Oliver doesn't have any children with his current wife and has always wanted a boy. He's hoping to raise Daniel as his own." He clicked off his phone. "We need to be extra vigilant. Evan failed this time, but he'll be back."

Both men nodded. They discussed strategies and came up with a plan to fortify the ranch further. Kyle was grateful for the help. Protecting both Sierra and Daniel would've been difficult on his own, given the level of the threat against them.

After Walker and Jason left the office, Kyle fired up his computer. He spent the next twenty minutes digging into Agent Jeff Lewis. It wasn't a thorough search, but it was enough to make him feel better about trusting the man. Kyle shoved away from the desk and, despite the late hour, headed into the kitchen for coffee. Sleep was a luxury he couldn't afford right now. There was too much to do.

He drew to an abrupt stop in the kitchen doorway and nearly burst out laughing. Sierra was busy mixing formula for Daniel. She'd obviously roped Tucker into holding the baby so she could prepare the bottle quickly. The former Army Ranger was frozen in place, Daniel nestled between his extended hands. The terrified expression etched on Tucker's face gave way to pure panic when the baby wriggled his tiny feet and gave a wail of unhappiness and hunger.

"Tucker, what on earth are you doing?" Kyle couldn't resist teasing his friend. "It's a baby, not a bomb."

Tucker shot him a scowl and muttered, "A bomb would be easier." He blinked and seemed to realize how his words could be taken. He tossed a sheepish glance toward Sierra. "No offense. This one seems cute, as far as kids go. Just...not for me."

Sierra laughed. "No offense taken."

Kyle took pity on the other man and extended his arms. "Here, give Daniel to me."

Relief washed over Tucker's face. He awkwardly, abet carefully, transferred the baby over. Then he murmured something about checking the perimeter before bolting toward the back door. Kyle wasn't surprised by his friend's swift exit. Tucker was a great guy, but he'd stated many times that he had no interest in family life. He hadn't gone into details as to why, and Kyle hadn't pushed. It was part of what made their support group work. Tucker would open up when and if he was ready.

Kyle bounced Daniel slightly to distract the baby from his hunger. "Who knew you could be so scary, little man?"

"I did." Sierra set the bottle on the kitchen table and then gently plucked the baby from Kyle's arms. She placed a kiss on Daniel's forehead. "There's nothing worse than a baby's cry. You want to do whatever you can to fix it."

She settled in a chair and started feeding Daniel. The baby gulped down his milk eagerly, eyes fixed on his aunt's face. He was so small and fragile. Innocent. Kyle was no stranger to responsibility, but this...it was something different altogether. The sniper attack at the coffee shop today drove home the level of danger they were facing. One wrong move and Sierra's life wouldn't be the only one changed forever.

Kyle was used to standing shoulder to shoulder with soldiers. Men and women who'd decided to put their lives on the line for their country. But Sierra hadn't chosen this. She'd been thrust into an impossible situation by her father, a man who should've cherished and taken care of her. It was horrific to think about.

After the sniper attack, Sierra hadn't fallen apart, which she would've had the right to do. She'd dusted the glass off her clothes and sprung into action, ensuring everyone else in the coffee shop was okay. Her actions had been both brave and impressive. And now, seeing her holding Daniel so sweetly after such an awful evening, tugged at Kyle's heartstrings.

Sierra glanced up. "Everything okay?"

"Yes and no." Kyle hated to add more troubles to Sierra's plate, but she deserved to know about the breach attempt on the ranch. He wouldn't withhold information or lie to her. Their conversation at the coffee shop about her childhood had struck a chord. He wanted to be someone she trusted, and that meant being honest, even when it was difficult. "While we were at the coffee shop, masked men tried to get onto the property. They failed. Jason and Logan responded to the threat, but unfortunately, the men escaped."

"Another kidnapping attempt." Sierra sighed and adjusted her hold on the bottle. "I'm not surprised."

Neither was Kyle. "The important thing is that the ranch security worked. I've spoken to Jason and Walker. We're going to increase patrols around the property. I don't want you to worry, but I also didn't want to hide what happened from you."

"I appreciate that. More than you know." Determination flared in her eyes. "I have to find the evidence Lucy uncovered. It's the only way to end this and keep Daniel safe."

Kyle nodded and poured a cup of coffee. "Have you had a chance to go through your sister's files?"

"Some. Nothing stands out, but I'll keep looking. If I can't uncover which company was laundering money, I may have to speak to Lucy's boss."

He joined her at the table. "We need to tread lightly. Someone tipped Oliver off to what Lucy was doing. We don't know who it was."

"It could've been Agent Lewis. He knew my sister's real identity. Her death should've raised a lot of red flags, but didn't. And then at the coffee shop, he claimed to be calling his boss, but Jeff could've easily contacted the sniper. The first shot was fired after he left the table."

"The same thought occurred to me, which is why I spent some time digging into Jeff's background." Kyle leaned back in his chair. "Born and raised here in Texas. 28 years old. Never married, no children. He attended the same university as your sister and graduated with honors. He's received several commendations during his eight years with the FBI. From what I can gather, he lives within his means. Jeff rents an apartment close to his office and has a Ford Taurus registered in his name."

"So if he's on Oliver's payroll, it's not obvious." Sierra frowned. Her brows creased in thought. "What about his family?"

"Parents are deceased. He's an only child. Oliver could've uncovered something in Jeff's past and is using that to force his cooperation, but if so, it's not readily apparent. I'll dig some more to be sure, but it looks like Agent Lewis is clean."

"Well, that's a relief." Sierra pulled the bottle from Daniel's mouth and shifted the baby to her shoulder. She patted his back gently. "But I still think we should stick to the plan. Whatever we uncover, we give it to Agent Lewis and Chief Garcia."

"Agreed." Kyle trusted Chief Garcia implicitly. The lawman would do everything in his power to help them. Trouble was, the police chief's jurisdiction ended at the Knoxville city line. He didn't have the power to fully investigate Oliver for crimes beyond their small town.

Taking down the entire Blackstorm organization was the only answer. Otherwise, Sierra and Daniel would never be safe. That wasn't an outcome Kyle was willing to entertain. He took another long sip of his coffee. "I'm not an accountant, but I know a thing or two about numbers. Would you like a hand looking at Lucy's files?"

Sierra smiled, the fatigue lifting from her expression. "I'd love that—"

Daniel let out a mighty burp. Sierra's eyes widened and then she burst out laughing. Kyle joined her. For one moment, he was able to forget about the sniper, Agent Lewis, and the threats from the hitmen. The warmth of the kitchen and the musical notes of Sierra's laugh surrounded him. He let it ease the tension from his muscles. Years in the battlefield had taught him to appreciate the joyful moments. They were fleeting and precious, especially when danger lurked so close.

How far would Oliver go to accomplish his goals? How much would he risk? Based on today's attacks, things were far from over. A storm was coming their way, deadly and intense. Kyle could feel it.

Please, God, help me protect them.

TWELVE

The elevator doors swished open and Sierra stepped into the gilded lobby of Watson's Accounting Service. The business was on the top floor of a skyscraper in downtown Austin. Midmorning sunshine streamed across the black marble floor. Comfortable couches were arranged around a coffee table with a fancy metal sculpture in the center. A waterfall fountain flowed down the wall behind the wide receptionist's desk.

Kyle stepped off the elevator next to Sierra. He'd dressed more formally today in a blazer and slacks, but paired the outfit with a brown cowboy hat. The man could grace a magazine cover, he was so gorgeous. It didn't help that a chiseled jawline and broad shoulders were only the beginning of his attractive qualities. Kyle was brave, kind, and loyal. Despite their agreement to keep things in the friend zone, Sierra's heart skipped a beat when he placed a hand on the small of her back to steer her across the lobby to the receptionist.

Bea James glanced up from the computer she was typing on. Her curly hair was tightly braided and bejeweled with clips. The stones matched the color of her silk blouse. Recognition flashed across Bea's face and then her eyes widened. "Sierra, hi."

"Hey, Bea." This wasn't Sierra's first visit to her sister's work-place. She'd often popped by to have lunch with Lucy and had gotten to know several members of the staff. Bea, in particular, had been someone Lucy considered a friend.

Sierra placed her hands on the desk. "Sorry to drop in without calling first, but I'd like to speak to Iris, if possible."

Iris Watson. Lucy's former boss. Sierra had spent most of last night and early this morning reviewing her sister's work files. There hadn't been anything suspicious. Coming to Austin was risky, espe-cially since her father was in the area, but Sierra didn't have a choice. The faster she located the evidence her sister had hidden, the sooner Oliver and his thugs would be locked behind bars.

"Is something wrong?" Bea asked, rising gracefully from her chair.

Sierra hesitated. Her automatic habit was to lie. There was no way to know who'd told Oliver about Lucy's investigation. Anyone—including Bea—could be on his payroll. But what difference would it make to hide it? Sierra was already on her father's radar. Sharing what she knew wouldn't change that. "There's an issue with one of Lucy's clients. It's important that I speak to Iris."

Concern flickered in Bea's eyes. "She had a phone conference scheduled this morning. Let me see if she's done."

"Thanks."

Bea disappeared into the back offices, her heels clicking against the marble floor. Kyle waited until she was out of earshot before saying, "You should take the lead in this meeting. Iris knows you and is more likely to answer your questions if I fade into the background."

Sierra snorted. "You clearly have no idea how much attention you attract. Iris isn't blind or deaf. There's no way you'll be able to fade into the background." She tilted her head toward a group of women tittering behind a nearby partition. Their coffee break had turned into a collective admiring. Not that Sierra could blame them.

A blush crept up Kyle's neck. Before he could say anything,

however, Bea reappeared and waved them back. They followed her to Iris's corner office. The door was open and Sierra's feet sank into the deep carpeting as she crossed the threshold. Stunning views of the city were visible beyond the floor-to-ceiling glass windows.

Iris stood behind her antique desk, perfectly at home among the expensive and elegant surroundings. Mid-forties, she was slender with the type of figure earned through eating salads rather than working out. Her Chanel suit was tailored to fit perfectly, and her hair was styled in flattering waves around an unlined face.

Sierra had met Iris several times and had always been impressed by the woman's business sense. She was wickedly smart. Watson Accounting had started as a small firm fifteen years ago, but now served some of the biggest companies in the state. To her knowledge, Lucy and Iris had always gotten along well.

"Sierra, it's so good to see you." Iris came around the desk to shake her hand. Her grip was firm but not overpowering. "I think of Lucy often. How's Daniel?"

"He's growing." Sierra was touched Iris asked about him. She released the older woman's hand and gestured toward Kyle. "This is my friend, Kyle Stewart."

Iris gave him an appreciative look before shaking his hand and exchanging pleasantries. Then she gestured to the silk-covered visiting chairs. "Please, have a seat. Bea mentioned there may be a problem with one of Lucy's clients. How can I help?"

Sierra selected one of the chairs and sat. "It's come to my attention Lucy may have uncovered something illegal prior to her death. She suspected one of her clients was laundering money."

Iris waved Bea out of the room and then shut the door to her office. "That's very concerning. I spoke with an FBI agent yesterday who alluded to the same thing. What makes you believe one of our clients is involved?"

"Your firm was the only one my sister worked for." Sierra had spoken with Jeff this morning and knew he'd interviewed Lucy's boss. He hadn't learned much however. Sierra wasn't willing to sit back and wait for the FBI to make progress. Not given the threats against her and Daniel.

She tilted her head. "Did Lucy ever share any concerns with you about a client?"

"Nothing along the lines of what you're saying."

That was deeply troubling. If Lucy didn't feel she could confide in her boss, there must've been a reason for it. Did her sister suspect Iris was involved? Or was she trying to shield the firm from bad publicity? Any connection to Blackstorm could send respectable clients fleeing. It would be devastating for business.

Iris dropped into her leather desk chair. Her perfectly plucked brows drew down in concern. "I'm shocked by these allegations, frankly. I'm going to tell you what I said to Agent Lewis. If any of our clients were involved in something illegal, we would cut them loose. There must be some mistake."

Sierra removed a printed list and set it on the desk. "Can you tell me if this is a complete list of my sister's clients?"

Iris picked up the paper. Her manicure was fresh, the nails painted blood red. She scanned the names. "These are all the ones I know about." She set the list down, her expression hardening into displeasure. "All of these businesses are legitimate, run by good and honest people. No one is laundering money. I certainly hope you don't intend to suggest otherwise."

"No. I would never accuse anyone without justification."

Iris didn't miss a beat. "That's wise. It would also be prudent to leave the investigation to the police." She glanced at her watch before rising. "Forgive me, but I have a meeting in five minutes that I must prepare for."

Frustration nipped at Sierra. Iris hadn't been helpful, and now she was stonewalling them. Sierra hated being suspicious of someone her sister had considered a friend, but the files on Lucy's computer hadn't yielded any leads. Iris had to be lying about the client list. Proving it, however, would be next to impossible.

Sierra hooked her purse over her shoulder. "Thank you for your time."

"Of course." Iris strolled to her office door but paused before opening it. "I was fond of your sister, so allow me to offer a bit of advice. Accusations of criminal behavior shouldn't be flung around lightly. If you aren't careful, you could get yourself into a lot of trouble."

Was that a threat? It sounded like one. From the way Kyle stiffened, he'd taken it the same way. Sierra's blood heated. She was sick of bullies. First her father and now Iris. She stepped closer to the older woman and held her gaze. "Allow me to offer you a bit of advice. The truth always comes out, Iris. Always."

Iris's nostrils flared as her eyes went flat and cold. She yanked her office door open with more force than was necessary. Sierra lifted her chin and marched out, anger fueling every one of her steps.

Kyle caught up with her in the hall. "That may not have been the smartest thing to do."

"Maybe not, but I already have a target on my back. I'm tired of running scared. I've been doing it my whole life." She shoved the door leading to the lobby open. The receptionist's desk was empty, as was the waiting room. Sierra jabbed at the elevator button. "Iris is hiding something. She's lying about my sister's client list."

High heels clipped behind them. Sierra spun around to find Bea hurrying in their direction. She was carrying several sack lunches. She tossed them on the receptionist desk before crossing to the elevator.

"I wanted to catch you before you left." Bea came to a breathless stop in front of Sierra. Her complexion was pale and beads of sweat were on her brow. She sucked in air, placing a hand on her chest. "Goodness, the cafeteria is three flights down, and I ran all the way there and back."

Sierra spotted a water cooler in the corner of the room. She filled a plastic cup with the cool liquid and handed it to Bea. "Here."

"Thanks." She drank and took another deep breath. "Better. I didn't want you to leave without getting the chance to say goodbye. It's not often we see each other." Bea glanced over her shoulder and then whispered, "Ask me to show you where the cafeteria is."

Sierra blinked. The request caught her completely off guard, but Bea took another drink of water, her brows raised expectantly. Lucy's friend was clearly up to something. Was there surveillance in the office? A listening device? It would explain Bea's strange behavior.

Sierra purposefully glanced at the lunch sacks sitting on the receptionist's desk. "Is the cafeteria in this building any good? I skipped breakfast and I'm starving."

"It's got a great tuna melt."

"Mind showing us where it is?"

Bea smiled. "Not at all." She waved to one of the other secretaries passing through. "I'm popping down to the cafeteria. Be back in a jiffy."

The elevator dinged, and the doors swished open. Kyle held his arm out to stop the elevator from closing until they were inside.

Once the car started moving, Bea hit the stop button to halt it. She spun toward Sierra. "Sorry for the subterfuge, but the entire office is wired for cameras and audio. I didn't want Iris finding out I'd requested to be alone with you. Jackson Construction. That's the client Lucy was investigating."

Sierra's breath caught. "Can you give me access to their records?"

Bea shook her head. "The morning after Lucy died, those files were erased from our database. It's like the client never existed as far as our system is concerned."

Things didn't get more suspicious than that. "What did Lucy tell you?"

"Only that Jackson Construction was doing something illegal and it was connected to Blackstorm." Tears filmed Bea's dark eyes. "Was she...was she murdered?"

Sierra's heart cracked at the tremble in the other's woman's voice. Bea's grief touched her own. "I believe so. But we're going to do everything we can to catch the people responsibility." She paused. "Do you believe Iris is involved?"

"I don't know. Things have been tense around the office since Lucy's death. Maybe Iris is afraid of bad publicity. She built the firm from the ground up and is very protective of it..." Bea swallowed hard. "To be honest, I've kept my head down and haven't asked questions. Blackstorm is a dangerous organization. I don't want word to get back to the wrong person that I was looking into things."

Sierra couldn't blame her. "Did Lucy say anything else to you about what she was investigating?"

"No, but your sister was smart. I'm sure she kept a copy of the Jackson Construction records somewhere."

Sierra agreed. The question was: where?

THIRTEEN

The parking garage for Watson Accounting was attached to the skyscraper through a breezeway over the street. Kyle kept his senses on high alert. If Iris was working with Blackstorm—and it seemed likely she was—then it would take one phone call to have Evan and his gang heading this way. Kyle had minutes to get Sierra to safety. Maybe seconds. The conversation with Bea had delayed their exit, but the information she'd provided had been invaluable.

Beside him, Sierra kept pace with his long strides. Kyle placed a hand on the small of her back, and his pulse quickened when she leaned into the touch. He liked being her protector. More than he should.

His phone beeped with an incoming message. Nathan. His cousin had been watching Kyle's vehicle while it was in the parking lot. Blackstorm would use any method to silence Sierra, including bombs or trackers. Since the vehicle was registered in his name, Kyle had to take extra precautions. His truck had been examined by Jason and Tucker in the bus terminal parking lot before they drove it to the ranch and then again after the incident with the sniper. It'd been clean, and Kyle was determined to keep it that way.

He lifted his arm to read the text message on his watch. All clear. Sierra cast a worried glance in his direction. "Everything okay?"

"Yes, but I'll feel better once we're out of here."

"That makes two of us."

The parking lot was dimly lit and smelled of gasoline. Kyle's truck sat in a visitor's spot close to the stairs. He hit the fob on his key ring and then opened the passenger door for Sierra. She got into the vehicle. Moments later, they were on the busy downtown street. Kyle spotted Nathan's vehicle behind them and breathed out a sigh of relief.

They were safe. For now.

Kyle's phone rang, and he answered using the hands-free system on his steering wheel. "Stewart."

"This is Agent Jeff Lewis. I've got some good news. We arrested George Sampson this morning. Based on the surveillance video we collected from the surrounding businesses yesterday, he was the sniper. George isn't talking, of course, but the federal prosecutor is working on making a deal with his attorney. We're hoping George will flip on Evan and Oliver in exchange for a lighter sentence."

Sierra's face flushed and her hands balled into fists. "A lighter sentence? That man shot into a coffee shop full of innocent people. It was a miracle he didn't kill or seriously injure anyone."

Jeff exhaled loudly. "I share your frustration. Don't forget, I was one of the people in that coffee shop with you. But this is how investigations work. The FBI has attempted several times to use undercover officers to infiltrate the organization and failed. Oliver keeps his inner circle very close. George is one of the few high-level members of Blackstorm we know about. The information he has is valuable, and if we can get him to talk, it'll help us dismantle the entire organization."

Kyle checked his mirrors. The freeway was mostly empty. No one other than Nathan appeared to be following them. "What are the chances George will flip?"

"I won't lie to you. It's not good. While my boss and the prosecutor are working on George, I'm going to keep pursuing other angles of the case. Have you found out any more information about Lucy's investigation?"

Sierra tucked a strand of dark hair behind her ear. "We have the name of the company she was looking into. Jackson Construction. Have you heard of it?"

"Yes. It's a huge company with offices all over the US, including Chicago." A tapping came over the line as if Jeff were banging a pen against his desk. "Construction companies are a good way to traffic things. Lots of trucks carrying goods and equipment across state lines and even into Mexico and Canada. Were you able to get your hands on their financials?"

"No. The company's information was swiped from the database. Someone at Watson Accounting doesn't want anyone to know Jackson Construction was ever a client of theirs. The owner, Iris Watson, may be working with Oliver."

"Not necessarily. She may have uncovered what Jackson Construction was doing on her own and got rid of them as a client. We've had other accounting firms do the same. Organized crime makes most people, especially accountants, very nervous. As it should."

Kyle tapped his thumb against the steering wheel. Had he misjudged Iris? It'd seemed like the woman was threatening Sierra in her office, but maybe she truly meant her words as a warning. Or maybe she was simply doing as Bea said and trying to protect the reputation of her business. "Why would Jackson Construction use an accounting firm to begin with? If the company is connected to Oliver, wouldn't they use his accountants?"

"It would make Blackstorm's involvement too easy to trace. Oliver has avoided prosecution thus far by being unpredictable. And careful. His companies pay their federal and state taxes. To be honest, I'm surprised Lucy found something hidden in the books. They're meticulous about covering their tracks."

"My sister was an excellent accountant." Pride filled Sierra's voice.

"Obviously." A noise came over the line that sounded like someone calling Jeff's name. He said something that was muffled, and then his voice became clear again. "I've got to run, but I'll dig into Jackson Construction and see what I can find. Stay safe."

Kyle hung up and steered his truck toward the exit directing them to Knoxville. They passed the familiar welcome sign posted at the city border. Another smaller billboard announced next month's upcoming Strawberry Festival. Normal life. It seemed so far away from what they were dealing with. Kyle remembered how difficult it was in the weeks after he returned home from deployment. His entire world had changed, but everyone else's was the same. It'd been bizarre.

In the passenger seat, Sierra was quiet, her attention on the scenery passing outside her window. Golden sunshine brushed across the curve of her profile. Her eyes were hidden behind giant sunglasses, but Kyle caught her swipe at a tear as it coursed down her cheek. That small movement was like a punch to his gut. It wasn't enough to protect Sierra. He wanted to be there for her, to help shoulder the grief and heartache she was carrying.

Kyle reached out and took her hand. "We're going to figure this out."

"I know." She interlaced their fingers and gave him a soft smile. "Sorry to be so weepy. I'm normally made of tougher stuff, but this..."

"It's a lot. Give yourself some grace, Sierra. You're grieving Lucy. That alone would be enough to knock anyone off their feet. Add in the responsibility of raising Daniel and the threats on your life and you have more than enough reason to be emotional." He spared a glance at her before focusing back on the road. "You don't have to be strong all the time. It's okay to lean on me. I'm not going anywhere."

"My sister loved strawberries."

The sign announcing the fair. Sierra had been paying attention to the scenery after all. Her voice was hollow and filled with pain. Kyle wished he wasn't driving and could pull her into his arms. He knew well what it was like to miss someone so much it hurt to breathe.

Sierra leaned against the headrest, her face turned toward him. "Lucy read romance books, hated roller coasters, and loved to pull pranks. She had a scar on her arm from sneaking onto an abandoned property with some friends as a teenager. I was the first person she called when she got engaged; I helped pick out her wedding dress and bought the pregnancy test when Lucy suspected she was pregnant with Daniel." She swiped at more tears running down her cheeks. "I was in the delivery room when that precious baby was born. I thought I knew everything about my sister. It turns out I didn't know her at all."

"She was protecting you."

"That wasn't her job." Sierra jabbed at her chest. "I'm the older sister. I've protected Lucy all her life. How could she hide this from me? I'm so angry, Kyle, and at the same time, I'm so proud of her. It's a mess, and I can't do anything with these emotions tearing me apart."

"You can talk about them. Pray. Those seem like small things, but it helps. The worst thing is to hold it all inside. I learned that the hard way." He squeezed her hand again. "Maisy's death rattled me. I hung on during my deployment, but once I was back stateside, I became reckless. Stupidly doing every death-defying activity available. Skydiving, hang gliding, BMX biking. A buddy dared me to race him on a four-wheeler and I took up the challenge." Kyle winced, remembering how dangerously he'd run the course. "I took a turn way too fast, flipped the four-wheeler. Busted my head open and nearly killed myself."

He wasn't proud of his actions, but he'd been in so much pain, he hadn't known how to handle it. "I was admitted to the veteran's hospital, and they stitched up my head and a nasty cut on my leg.

Nathan was already there, recovering from injuries he'd received while on deployment. I met Jason. They encouraged me to open up about the struggles I was going through. I'm sure those guys saved my life."

"I'm glad you had them. The world is a better place with you in it, Kyle."

"I know that now." His mouth twitched. "Of course, Nathan and Jason weren't too happy with me when I saved Ms. Whiskers from a trashcan. I snuck her into the hospital and she secretly lived in our room for a few days before I was released."

Sierra's mouth dropped open and then she burst out laughing. "You didn't!"

"I did. Ms. Whiskers was the cutest kitten in the world, and as much as Nathan and Jason complain about her, I know they loved her too. The doctors and nurses must've known what we were up to, but they never said anything."

The road curved, and Knoxville creek came into view. A wooden bridge with yellow railings was the only way to cross it. The city had added a foot and bicycle path, since people loved to park on the side of the road and explore the forested park abutting the road. Several cars were tucked in the trees. The sunny spring weather had enticed more than one hiker out today.

Kyle slowed as he approached the bridge. He glanced in the rearview mirror, but Nathan's truck wasn't visible. His cousin had been keeping his distance in order to watch for anyone following them. The bends in the road prevented a clear line of sight.

Movement from the left caught his attention. Evan stepped out of the forest, something in his hand. Kyle reacted without thinking. His foot hit the gas as he grabbed Sierra's head and shoved it toward her lap.

An explosion blasted from their right as the car closest to the bridge blew up. Shards of glass flew in all directions as every window in Kyle's truck shattered simultaneously. Pain vibrated through him, too overwhelming to fully register. Heat followed. The force of the blast sent his vehicle skidding across the wooden slates. Kyle gripped the steering wheel, desperate to maintain control, but it was no use. The guardrail loomed large. Metal crunched and Kyle's belt jerked his shoulder as his vehicle slammed into the barrier. It broke, and the truck tipped.

"Sierra!" Kyle reached for her. Blood ran down the side of her face, but she was conscious. Her mouth moved. The roar of the explosion had damaged his hearing. For one heart stopping moment, the vehicle hovered on the edge of the bridge. Water rushed past them in the creek below.

Then they fell.

FOURTEEN

Ice cold.

Sierra's eyes snapped open. Frigid water surrounded her, pouring in through the shattered windows at an alarming rate. In moments, the vehicle would be completely submerged. Nothing looked right. It took her far too long to realize she was hanging upside down. The car had flipped, landing in the water with its wheels facing the sky.

Goose bumps covered her arms and her lungs burned. Sierra realized she must've instinctively drawn in a breath before they hit the water. The force of their fall had torn her hands from Kyle's. She fumbled with the seat belt, attempting to get her frozen fingers to coordinate enough to press the release button. Panic set in as the latch refused to let go.

A strong hand clamped over her wrist.

Kyle.

She turned her head in time to see him slice through her belt with a knife. The pressure against her shoulder released, and she floated in the water. Kyle snagged her hand and pulled her through the shattered windshield and into the rushing current of the creek. The cold sank into her bones. Everything felt muddled and slow.

Air. She needed air. Sierra kicked with her feet, struggling to lift her body through the water to the surface. Her clothes weighed her down. She could not die this way. She refused. Daniel needed her. Sierra urged one last burst of power into her legs, and coupled with Kyle's powerful grip, she broke the surface of the river and gasped in a desperate breath. Sweet oxygen filled her lungs.

An arm wrapped around her waist. Sierra clung to Kyle as the water swirled around them, threatening to batter their bodies against the protruding rocks. His mouth moved, but she couldn't make out the words. Her heart thundered in her chest. She couldn't catch her breath and her vision blurred. She was hyperventilating. Her self-defense training had included a course on reactions to life-threatening situations. Panic was one of them.

Sierra forced herself to take one deep breath and then another. She dug her fingers into Kyle's hard shoulder. His grip around her waist was firm, his hard body a warm refuge in the freezing water. With a jolt, she realized that he alone was keeping them afloat. His legs churned underneath the water. He pointed in a direction and Sierra nodded to show she understood his request. Together, they swam at an angle to the tree-lined shore. The bridge and their vehicle were no longer visible. They'd drifted too far downstream, the woods in this area unfamiliar and devoid of people.

The water became shallow. Her legs trembled as Sierra hauled herself the last few meters to safety. She collapsed against the ground. Grass tickled her cheek and the scent of damp earth and wet leaves embraced her. Sierra panted from exertion. "Thank you, God."

"You can say that again." Kyle's hand touched the back of her neck. It was warm against her chilled skin. "Are you hurt?"

She rolled over to face him. Water dripped from his hair, down his forehead, and along the column of his neck. His cheek was scraped and bleeding slightly. His boots were missing, as was his blazer, revealing a white T-shirt that molded over every ridge of his muscles. The worry in his gorgeous brown eyes nearly undid her. Had anyone ever looked at her that way? With such tenderness?

No. No one ever had. Her breath stalled as her pulse kicked up a notch. But this time, it wasn't from fear or panic.

Desire. It crashed into her with all the force of the water battering against the rocks nearby. Denying it was impossible. The spark ignited when they were teenagers so long ago had laid dormant, but it'd never been extinguished. Sierra had the most insane urge to lean forward and press her lips against his.

A twig cracked. Kyle's head snapped up a moment before something whizzed by them. Bark blew off a nearby pine tree as something thunked into it.

A bullet.

Someone was shooting at them.

Sierra was already scrambling to her feet before she was conscious of the movement. Kyle grasped her wrist and tugged her into the shelter of the forest. He pushed her ahead of him, using his body to protect her from the shooter. "Run, Sierra."

She bolted. Her tennis shoes slid over pine needles and leaves coating the ground. Roots jutted up, threatening to plunge her back to the ground. Her legs were unsteady, her breaths shallow. Wind whistled as more bullets flew past her. Close. Too close. A man shouted and another answered. They were being hunted like prey.

Kyle's footsteps pounded behind her. Prayers echoed in her heart as Sierra shoved branches out of the way. Sweat dripped down her back. The thick tree cover blocked out the sun. It made traversing the forest even harder.

How far had they gone? She wasn't sure. The ground rose in a steady incline. An outcropping of rocks appeared on the left. Sierra recognized it from her many hikes through these woods as a teenager. There was a road about half a mile away. If they could get there, a passerby could pick them up and drive them to the police station. Sierra hauled in a breath and turned.

She gasped. Kyle's shirt was covered in blood. His complexion was pale, his teeth gritted in pain. "Keep going."

He'd been shot and hadn't uttered a word. Sierra hurried to his side just as Kyle stumbled. Sweat beaded on his forehead as his hand shot out to grab a tree branch. He swayed but still managed to glare at her. "I said keep going."

"Until you collapse?" Sierra rolled her eyes and then ducked under his good arm. "Lean on me. We can hide in that rock outcropping. It's high ground, and we'll see anyone coming our way. By now, Nathan will have alerted the police that we went over the bridge. Chief Garcia will organize a search. They'll find us soon."

Her words were confident, although she was anything but. The shooters were still out there in the forest and nightfall was coming quickly. It would hinder the chief's search party. Kyle had made it this far by sheer strength of will, but he'd lost a lot of blood in the process. If they didn't address his wound now, he might not make it. Sierra refused to let him die when she could help.

Kyle grumbled, but when they reached the outcropping, he nearly collapsed to the ground. His skin was ghost white. Everything Sierra knew about first aid flashed through her mind. She shucked her long-sleeved shirt and used her teeth to tear the fabric into strips. It was dirty from the tumble in the lake and the run through the forest, but it was all she had.

She reached for the bottom of Kyle's shirt, but he waved her off, using his good hand to remove his cell phone from his pocket. The screen was shattered. He pushed a button on the side and nothing happened. Kyle groaned. "It's busted."

"That's not a surprise." Sierra hadn't replaced her own cell phone since leaving it in her home after the first attack. Probably a mistake, but now wasn't the time to consider it. She scowled. "Now, hold still so I can look at your wound." Sierra gently lifted the edge of his shirt. The hard plane of his flat stomach was coated in blood and sweat. A slice cut across the length of Kyle's midsection. It looked deep and painful.

He glanced down at it and glowered. "It's just a graze."

Kyle attempted to shove himself up, but Sierra put a hand on his chest to stop him. "It's a nasty one, tough guy, and if you don't hold still, you're going to bleed out right here. Then I'm going to put died-of-stupid-machoism on your tombstone."

For a moment, it looked like he was going to continue arguing with her. Then his shoulders sagged as he let out a breath. "Fine. Let's bind up the wound and keep moving." Kyle removed his gun from the holster at the small of his back. Water dripped from the metal and he made a face. "This probably won't do us much good after being soaking in the river. We're sitting ducks if Evan and his men find us."

"I haven't heard them for a while." Sierra laid several strips of fabric against Kyle's wound. The blue fabric turned dark with his blood. She needed to keep him conscious and talking. "Evan programmed a car bomb. That's what set us into the river, isn't it?"

Kyle nodded. "I should've realized..." He winced as she wrapped another long piece of fabric around his waist. "It's a trick I've seen in Afghanistan. I'm sorry, Sierra. I considered the potential of a car bomb on my vehicle, but I didn't think they'd use their own car to run us off the road."

"I don't want to hear you apologize again." She paused in her ministrations to hook a finger under his chin, lifting it until Kyle was forced to meet her gaze. "The only reason I'm alive is because of you. None of this is your fault. None of it."

His lips parted and then curved upward into a smile. "You missed your calling, Sierra. You would've made an excellent drill instructor. I didn't know you were so bossy."

"Neither did I." She'd buried her feelings and thoughts for so long behind a wall, it was refreshing to allow them to run free. It was the only silver lining in this whole mess. Well, that and her friendship with Kyle.

She wrapped more of her shirt around Kyle's waist and then knotted the end. "Logan won't be impressed by my skills as a field medic, but at least the bleeding has slowed."

That earned her another heart-stopping smile. "You underestimate yourself. I think Logan will be very impressed to learn you practically dragged me to these rocks and forcibly treated me. I'm not the easiest patient."

She rolled her eyes. "You don't say."

Kyle stiffened and then raised a finger to his lips. Sierra froze. A flock of birds took off from a nearby copse of trees, their cries a warning of potential trouble. The sun had completely disappeared behind the horizon. In the valley below them, the woods were a tangle of dark branches and deep hollows big enough to hide a person. Or people. Men with guns bent on killing Sierra and anyone who was with her.

Helpless. That's what she was. Unable to protect herself or Kyle. The feeling made her sick and angry all at once. Sierra didn't want to be this person, not anymore.

Kyle stifled a groan as he righted himself and leaned against the rock to peer down into the valley. His mouth was a hard line of determination. He held their water-logged gun, probably hoping it would still fire even after being drenched in the lake.

Sierra joined him and whispered, "Do you still have your knife?"

He silently removed it from a sheath attached to his belt and handed it to her. Sierra gripped the handle, letting the texture ridges dig into the soft flesh of her palm. The blade was little protection from a sniper's rifle, but it was something. It was a fighting chance.

Sierra was done running. She was tired of being terrorized. For far too long, she'd allowed fear to dictate her life choices and stayed in the shadows. Not anymore. From this moment on, if she survived, Sierra was going to use her strength to serve others. She would live a passionate life, raise Daniel to have integrity, make deep friendships, find a man to love and get married. She would become who God had created her to be.

Leaves rustled. Someone was coming toward them.

Sierra held her breath and waited for the enemy to show himself.

FIFTEEN

Kyle hated hospitals.

Rain lashed against the window, the raging thunderstorm matching his mood. He couldn't wait to escape from the drab room and the constant poking and prodding. It hadn't helped that he'd spent the entire night fretting about Sierra. Her injuries from the accident and the shooting had been minor, thank God. She'd returned to the ranch with Tucker and Jason after being released from the hospital.

Kyle winced as he shrugged on his shirt. The stitches along his side tugged with every movement and his head ache from being rammed against the car door during the tumble into the river. "How long does it take to prepare discharge paperwork?"

Nathan snorted. "You've driven the nurses and doctors crazy since arriving at the ER. Trust me, they're ready to give you a swift boot on the behind as you leave."

"That's because I didn't need to be admitted. I should've gone home last night with Sierra."

"Sure, sure. Thirty stitches across your abdomen and a concussion is nothing to worry about." He smirked. "I don't see why you're so eager to get back to the ranch. You aren't good for much in your condition. Sierra would be better off with Ms. Whiskers as a bodyguard."

Kyle balled up his hospital gown and threw it at his cousin's head. "I could have one foot in the grave and still be able to toss your butt to the floor. Wanna try me?"

"And risk the wrath of Aunt Gerdie? Uh, no." Nathan tossed the hospital gown on the nightstand. His smile widened. "You don't frighten me, but she does." His expression grew serious. "Sierra is fine. She's well-protected."

She was. Kyle knew that. But it didn't stop his mind from turning over dozens of scenarios like a constant reel of horror movies. They'd barely escaped Evan and his thugs yesterday. The attacks were well-planned. And deadly.

A knock on the doorframe preceded Chief Garcia into the room. His uniform was wrinkled, mud coated his boots, and he sported a five o'clock shadow. The dark circles under his eyes matched his grim expression. "Morning, boys. Kyle, how are you feeling?"

"Ready to get home." He finished the last button on his shirt and then planted his hands on his hips. He felt naked without his gun holstered at the small of his back and his knife on his belt. Both weapons were forbidden in the hospital.

"Can't blame you." The chief's nose wrinkled. "I ain't too fond of hospitals myself. But I'm glad you're back on your feet."

"Thank you, sir. What can you tell me about the status of the investigation?"

"Still ongoing." Chief Garcia removed a notepad from the front pocket of his shirt. "Witnesses identified Evan, along with two other men, in the area minutes prior to the car explosion. The bomb was homemade and remote detonated by a cell phone. After the accident, Evan's accomplices walked the riverbank to ensure you were dead."

"Except we survived. Which is when they started shooting."

Kyle's fingers twitched, and he was tempted to ball his hands into fists and punch something. Anything.

The chief nodded and then jerked his chin in Nathan's direction. "Your cousin saved the day. He called Jason, who came to the riverbank with Connor immediately. It's the reason we found y'all so quickly."

Connor was a retired bomb-sniffing dog, but Jason had been training him in search-and-rescue. Kyle made a mental note to buy a steak for the pup when this was all over. As difficult as it was to admit, if Evan's thugs had found them first, Kyle would've been outgunned and, given his physical condition, unable to protect Sierra. It'd been a relief to see Connor and then Jason emerge from the tree line.

Actually, no. When this was done, Kyle was throwing a party for everyone. He owed his friends, and Chief Garcia, an enormous debt of gratitude.

"I'm working closely with the FBI on this case." Chief Garcia closed his notebook and tucked it back inside his shirt pocket. "Agent Lewis has been very helpful. I made some phone calls—quietly, mind you—to ask some colleagues about him. No one had a bad word to say."

Kyle rocked back on his heels. That supported his own research on Jeff. Despite the agent's mistakes in the aftermath of Lucy's accident, it seemed he could be trusted. "Has there been any progress in getting George to flip?"

"Not to my knowledge. Jeff is also going to question Iris Watson again."

"I suspect she may be involved with Blackstone. It's possible Iris tipped Evan off yesterday as we were leaving Austin."

"It's also conceivable that Evan and his band of merry felons were simply lying in wait for you to cross the bridge. It's the primary route in and out of Knoxville. We'll know more once we're further into the investigation." Chief Garcia pegged him with the look. "In the meantime, do me a favor. Try not to get shot again."

Kyle chuckled. "That's the plan, sir."

The men shook hands and then the chief left. A few moments later, the nurse came in with the discharge paperwork. Kyle signed everything without a second glance and barely paid attention to the wound care instructions. When he finally exited the hospital, relief washed over him. The feeling deepened once they were on the road.

Nathan punched a button on the radio station and country music filled the cab. "I hope you don't mind stopping by Nelson's to pick up some pies. Your mom called in an order and I offered to pick it up for her since we were passing by there."

Frustration flared at the delay in seeing Sierra, but Kyle tamped it down. His mom had a houseful of men to feed. "Sure thing."

Fifteen minutes later, they pulled into the parking lot at Nelson's Diner. Harriet spotted their vehicle and hurried out, a tower of pie boxes in her hands. Kyle's mouth dropped open as Nathan got out to assist her. "How many did my mom order? Are we feeding the entire town?"

Nathan smirked. "Practically. You should see the crowd at the house."

Harriet patted Kyle's arm through the open window. "You're the talk of the town today, hon. Heard all about your troubles. I'm glad you and that sweet young lady are safe." She winked. "I included a pecan pie in the order just for you."

She was a treasure. Ignoring the pulling of his stitches, Kyle leaned out and kissed her cheek. "Give my best to Nelson."

"Will do." Harriet gave a last wave and hurried back inside.

Nathan hopped back in the driver's seat and shoved the truck into Drive. "Let's get home. Aunt Gerdie promised to make her famous pulled pork and mashed potatoes. I'm starving."

Kyle's stomach growled. He couldn't remember the last time he'd eaten. The enticing aromas of the pies didn't help matters, and when they arrived at the ranch, he barely waited for Nathan to stop the truck before getting out.

The front door swung open and Sierra burst out of the house. Kyle's heart leapt. Everything melted away as their gazes met across the distance between them. Relief flickered across her gorgeous features, but it was mixed with something else, something he couldn't name but made his pulse kick up higher and quickened his gait.

Sierra flew down the porch steps on bare feet. Her arms opened as if she was about to launch herself into his embrace, but at the last moment, she skid to a stop. Worry dimmed her smile. "I don't want to hurt your stitches."

Kyle wasn't having it. He closed the distance between them and pulled Sierra into his arms. She melted against him with a sigh, her cheek resting on his chest. He breathed in the scent of her perfume, soft and feminine, and let it soothe the raw edges of his nerves. "You okay?"

"Me." She pulled back to look him in the face. "I'm fine. You're the one who nearly bled to death."

"Don't mind me," Nathan hollered as he passed them, his arms full of pie boxes. "I'm just the dude who donated the blood to save his life, stayed with him in the hospital, and is now stuck carrying all the dessert."

Kyle didn't even glance at his cousin. "Whiner."

Sierra laughed. She backed out of Kyle's embrace but kept an arm around his waist. He didn't want to think about how right it felt to have her by his side. A pang of guilt tried to wedge its way into the moment, but Kyle battled it back. He and Sierra were just friends. They'd bonded over the last few days in the same way that soldiers on the battlefield did, but it didn't go beyond that. His heart still belonged to Maisy.

Tucker hopped down the steps of the porch on an intercept path with Nathan but tossed a grin toward Kyle. His teeth were bright white against the surrounding red beard. "Sierra won't say anything, so I'll do the bragging for her. She's a better shot than you, army brat. Maybe after dinner, we can head to the range."

Kyle had converted an old barn into a shooting range years ago. He arched his brows and looked down at Sierra. "You learned how to shoot?"

She nodded, a triumphant smile on her beautiful face. "Tucker's a good teacher."

"The best teacher," he hollered in reply. "She shot a bulls-eye before our first lesson was over."

Kyle wanted to ask how many lessons they'd had while he was in the hospital, but Gerdie stepped onto the porch before he could. Daniel was nestled in her arms. The little boy was wrapped in a soft blue blanket the same color as his eyes. Kyle kissed his mother's cheek and then smiled down at the little boy. Warmth spread through his chest. "I know it's only been twenty-four hours, but he looks bigger to me. Is that nuts?"

"Not at all. Babies this age grow so fast." Gerdie tilted her head toward the door. "I hope you're hungry because the food is ready. Word of warning, it's a full house. Everyone wanted to be here to greet you when you got home from the hospital."

Kyle followed his mom and Sierra inside. Instantly, he understood why his mom had ordered so many pies. All of his friends were there, along with Cassie, Nathan's wife, and Addison, Jason's wife. The next few minutes were spent saying hello before his dad ordered everyone to sit down. The dining room table was covered in food.

"Please join hands for grace." Rob bowed his head once everyone had done as requested. "Lord, we thank you for gathering us here today to share this meal together. Recent events serve as a reminder that friends and loved ones are the most precious things in our lives. We ask that you continue to watch over us, especially Sierra and Daniel. In your name we pray. Amen."

A chorus of "Amens" followed. The meal was rowdy, full of hilarious stories and laughter. Daniel passed from one set of loving arms to another. Sierra traded barbs with Nathan and teased Tucker. From the look of things, she fit right in with Kyle's friends and their wives. It made his heart happy to see her laugh so much. Especially given the stress she'd been under.

Ms. Whiskers twined her way around Kyle's legs, and he fed pieces of pulled pork to her under the table. Connor rose from his bed in the corner and trotted over, hoping to get his own treat. Kyle snuck him some of the meat too before patting his head. "Thanks for rescuing us, buddy."

After dinner, guests pitched in to clear the dishes. Sierra rose to help, but everyone waved her down. Kyle appreciated the way his friends looked out for her. Although Sierra's injuries weren't serious, she had to be sore and achy from yesterday's attack.

She settled back into her chair with a sigh and patted her belly. "I overindulged, but it was too good to resist."

Connor nosed her hand and she absently reached down to pet him while casting a narrowed gaze in Kyle's direction. "How on earth do you manage to stay in such good shape? If I lived with your mom, you'd have to roll me out the door."

He chuckled. "Ranch work." Ms. Whiskers attempted to swipe at the dog with her claws extended. Jealous thing. Kyle placed the cat in his lap and then scratched behind her ears. She immediately responded with a loud purr.

Sierra tilted her head toward the opposite side of the dining room. "Check out Addison and Jason."

The couple were cooing over the baby. Jason, the tough and hardened Marine, had Daniel in his arms and was rocking from side to side. He planted a kiss on his wife's lips and said something that made her chuckle. It was a sweet and tender moment. Intimate. And it tugged at all the loneliness Kyle had been avoiding dealing with since Maisy's death.

He'd wanted a family. Marriage. Kyle believed all of those desires had died with his fiancée, but here they were, flaring to life. And it was almost too painful to put into words.

"Daniel hasn't been put down all afternoon." Sierra shook her head, but a soft smile played on her lips. "Your friends are amazing. I love all of them..." The happiness melted from her face. She placed a hand on his arm. "Hey, are you okay?"

No. He wasn't okay. Suddenly, the room felt too hot and Sierra's touch seemed to brand his skin, but Kyle didn't know how to put into words what he was feeling. He wasn't even sure it was a wise idea to share his runaway thoughts. Sierra had enough problems on her plate. She didn't need to add his momentary emotional meltdown to the mix.

His cell phone beeped with a notification, saving him from having to reply to her question. Kyle pulled it out and glanced at the screen. Someone was requesting permission to enter through the front gate. Every muscle in his body tensed when he flipped to the camera.

"What is it?" Sierra asked.

He lifted his gaze to hers. "Your father. He's here."

SIXTEEN

Sierra gripped the roll bar of Nathan's truck as they drove past peaceful fields of wildflowers and grazing horses to the front gate. The sun was setting on the horizon, painting the sky with rich purple and pale yellows. Kyle reached across the back seat of the truck and took her hand. She interlocked their fingers, the warmth of his skin and the strength of his touch grounding her. She wasn't alone. Trouble and danger had found Sierra, but God had sent a fierce protector to defend her. And she was never more grateful to have Kyle next to her than at this moment.

Something was happening between them. Despite their agreement to keep the relationship in the friend zone, Sierra was tipping perilously close to losing her heart to the handsome veteran at her side. It was awful timing, and the future was uncertain, but these feelings she had for Kyle grew with every second in his presence. She didn't have the foggiest notion how to handle them, but now wasn't the time to think about it. Not when Sierra was about to speak to her criminal father for the first time since fleeing her childhood home in the middle of the night.

A man whose blood she shared.

A man who'd repeatedly tried to kill her.

The bitter taste of fear filled Sierra's mouth and a shudder rippled through her body. The habitual instinct to run clawed her insides. It was sheer strength and a newfound determination that kept her from yelling to turn the truck around before they reached the gate.

Kyle gently squeezed her hand. "You don't have to do this. Nathan and I can handle your father."

From the driver's seat, Nathan gave a sharp nod. The men had quickly created a plan before leaving the house. Jason, Logan, and Walker were sneaking through the property to approach the ranch gate from different angles. Tucker stayed at the house to protect Daniel, in case Oliver's arrival was a strategic diversion designed to distract from a covert attack by his hitmen. Chief Garcia had been called as well. Police officers were en route to the house. Not that Oliver could be arrested. He hadn't trespassed, and so far, the attacks on Sierra couldn't be linked to him. Yet.

Sierra pulled in a bracing breath. "I appreciate the support, but Oliver is here to see me. I won't give him the satisfaction of seeing me hide or cower like a terrified little girl." She jutted up her chin, letting the anger and defiance erase her fear. "He sees me as weak. I'm not."

"No, you aren't." Kyle's eyes shimmered with pride. "And anyone who'd been on that mountain yesterday would've noticed. Nathan, did I tell you Sierra took my knife and faced the potential oncoming danger like a warrior? She nearly scared Jason and Connor half to death when they popped out of the tree line."

Despite the trouble ahead, she laughed. "I think it was the blood covering my hands from dressing your wound that frightened Jason, not my warrior stance."

Kyle shook his head. "Nope. It was you."

A warmth filled her insides at the conviction layering his words. It silenced the last whisper of doubt about her decision to confront her father head on. She could do this. She *would* do this.

Nathan took a final bend in the road and the ranch gate came into view. A large SUV was sitting at an angle, as if the driver was prepared to flee if necessary. The rear windows were dark, making it impossible to see how many individuals were inside. Oliver stood in the open wearing a designer gray suit. Sunglasses shielded his eyes. Pushing sixty, he had the physique of a man half his age. Everything about him screamed money and power.

Memories she didn't want rushed Sierra. The feel of his hand on her cheek, the faint impression of bedtime stories and giant hugs. The moment he shot her dog. Good and the evil recollections jumbled together in a conflicting mix coated with pain and confusion. Sierra imagined shoving each of those thoughts into a box and locking it closed. This moment required every ounce of her strength.

"Get out of the car on my side," Kyle instructed, squeezing her hand once more before releasing it. He opened the rear door of the extended cab and a sweet breeze wafted into the vehicle. It smelled of wildflowers and honeysuckle. The grass was wet from the recent thunderstorm.

Sierra followed Kyle out of the truck, and he took a protective posture on her right. Nathan joined them on her left and then hit a button on a portable fob to open the gate. It swung inward soundlessly.

Oliver removed his sunglasses. His piercing blue eyes—the same shade as Sierra's own—flickered over her. "So it is true. You're alive, Jacqueline."

Her real name on his lips was jolting. She halted several arm lengths away. "I am alive. No thanks to you." She forced herself to meet his gaze. "I think we can skip the fake surprise and false pleasantries. What do you want?"

He tsk-tsked. "Such a horrible way to greet your father. I can only imagine the lies your mother spun to turn you against me. After Gwen kidnapped you, I hired private investigator after private investigator." He held a hand to his heart. "Not a day has gone by that I haven't thought of you."

I'll bet. Oliver was doing his best to sound like a loving father, but Sierra wasn't buying it. Oh, she believed he'd hired private investigators to find them. But not to reconcile. Sierra may have only been a child when she left with her mother, but Sierra hadn't cried out that night. Nor did she attempt to contact Oliver in the months and years afterward. She'd sided with her mother. It was a betrayal, one he would never tolerate, especially from his own flesh and blood.

What was he doing here? What was Oliver's game? Arriving at the ranch unexpectedly had to be part of a strategy, but for the life of her, Sierra couldn't figure out what he had to gain from it. She licked her lips. "What do you want, Oliver?"

A pained look creased his features. "There's no need for formality. Or bodyguards. I'm your father, Jacqueline. I would never hurt you, despite what you may have heard from others. It's been such a long time. I was hoping we could talk."

The rear door of the SUV opened. Kyle stiffened as he took a step forward, shielding Sierra with his body. She angled her head to see around him. Oliver's wife, Cece, exited the vehicle, looking like a movie star in a calf-length dress that swirled around her legs as she came to stand next to her husband. A diamond the size of a robin's egg decorated her left ring finger, and more jewels sparkled from her neck and earrings.

Cece placed a hand on her husband's arm, but her gaze locked on Sierra. "Your father is telling you the truth. He was overjoyed to discover you're okay, although we were heartbroken to hear of Lucy's accident. Please, there's no need to speak in the driveway like strangers. Let's go up to the house. We can explain everything there and it'll give us a chance to meet Daniel."

With a sudden jolt, the reason for their arrival became crystal clear. Daniel. They wanted to see the baby. A white, hot protectiveness raced through her veins. It was so potent, Sierra shook from the force of the emotion. "If you think I'm going to let either of you within ten yards of Daniel, you're delusional."

Oliver sighed, as if the weight of the world rested on his shoulders. He shook his head. "I'd hoped it wouldn't come to this, but you've left me no choice." He reached inside the pocket of his suit and pulled out a pack of folded pages. He tossed them on the ground. "You can't keep Daniel from me."

Confusion melted the edges of her anger. Kyle stepped forward and retrieved the papers. He scanned the documents and then his hand crumpled the pages. "This is impossible."

"What?" Sierra demanded.

Oliver's lips curved into a confident smile. "I've filed in family court for custody of Daniel. As his biological grandfather, I have legal rights." He patted Cece's hand, which was still resting on his arm. "And we can provide a safe and loving home for him."

She gaped, unable to fully process what he was saying. It was preposterous. "No judge in their right mind would give you custody. You're the leader of Blackstorm. A criminal and a killer."

If he was upset or surprised by her accusation, none of it showed in his expression. Oliver remained nonchalant, a smirk lingering on his lips. "You've been listening to rumors, dear. I'm a proper business man. Nothing more. Any judge will see it."

"You were on trial for murder until last week."

Cece laughed. "And he was acquitted."

They were going to buy the judge off. Or use some other nefarious means to sway the custody trial in their direction. Oliver intended to get his hands on Daniel by legal or illegal means. Sierra's hands balled into fists as the temptation to close the distance between them overcame her. Her vision narrowed to Oliver's smirk. She took a step forward, her body shaking with anger as reason fled. She was a mama protecting her young.

Kyle's arm looped around her waist, holding her in place. "Don't," he whispered in her ear. "They'll use it against you."

Sierra blinked, the rage-induced mist clearing from her vision. Two Knoxville squad cars had arrived at the ranch. The police officers stood next to their vehicles, standing ready to assist should Oliver start trouble. If Sierra clocked him, she'd be arrested for assault.

Embarrassment heated her cheeks. Was she any better than her father? It triggered Sierra's deepest fears about herself, that maybe a violent nature coursed through her veins. Her gaze met Oliver's. His smirk widened as if he'd heard her thoughts.

No. She refused to be anything like him.

"I'm okay," she whispered, her self-control restored. Kyle released her and Sierra straightened her shoulders. "You can file for custody, but you won't win. Lucy and her husband made a will. I'm Daniel's legal guardian, and that's exactly how it will stay."

"We'll see." Oliver's tone remained pleasant, but his eyes became like blue flint. "Be careful, dear. I've heard about the close calls you've had recently with some ruffians your sister crossed. I'd hate for anything to happen to you."

Kyle snorted. "There's no need to worry. I won't let anyone harm her." His tone was confident and coated with steel. "And as long as there is breath in my body, you'll never get your hands on Daniel."

Oliver's expression morphed into sheer hatred. "Don't make promises you can't keep."

"It's not a promise, it's a guarantee. Now get off my land before I have these officers forcibly remove you."

SEVENTEEN

Frustration pulsed through Kyle's veins as he stood in the kitchen impatiently waiting for Addison to finish reading the documents Oliver left. Her blond hair fell like a curtain as she bent over the papers. A pad and pen sat at her elbow.

As a family law attorney, Addison understood and could explain the implications of Oliver's custody claims. Jason sat next to his wife, a scowl puckering the scar along his cheek, a discarded cup of coffee resting on the table in front of him. Logan and Tucker were patrolling the property. Oliver's arrival at the gate hadn't resulted in another attack, but they wouldn't lower their guard for a moment.

Sierra paced the length of the kitchen next to the large bay window. She held Daniel in her arms. The baby fussed and wriggled, periodically tossing the pacifier out of his mouth to let loose a wail. Even he seemed to sense the tension in the room. Gerdie hovered at the kitchen counter, pouring more coffee into mugs and slicing pie. Kyle couldn't think of eating or drinking anything but accepted the plate his mother offered anyway. She was doing her best to comfort them.

Addison flipped to the last page in the stack of documents and scribbled a final note before looking up. "Okay, here's what I can tell you. As Daniel's biological grandfather, under Texas law, he may request visitation. He can also file, as he's done here, for custody since Lucy and her husband are deceased."

Gerdie gasped and placed a trembling hand to her mouth. "To think of Daniel in that man's care..."

"It won't happen." Kyle had sworn a vow to protect Sierra and Daniel until his last breath. That included fighting Oliver in the court system if necessary.

God, things are taking a turn. I could use Your help and guidance here.

Sierra joined them at the table, patting Daniel's back and swaying. "But Lucy and her husband named me as Daniel's guardian in their will."

"And their instructions will go a long way with the judge, but that's not a guarantee, unfortunately." Addison tapped the stack of documents. "Oliver is claiming that you're unfit to raise Daniel based on your inability to keep him safe over the last few days."

Kyle glowered. "He's the reason they're in danger in the first place."

"I'm with you, but we can't prove that." Addison held up a hand to ward off his next statement. "If you're asking my professional opinion, I don't think Oliver can gain full custody of Daniel, but visitation is a real possibility. Based on what we know so far, I believe he filed this petition for a few reasons. One, he establishes a desire to raise Daniel before Sierra is killed, thereby clearing the way for him to gain custody after her death. And two, he wanted to rattle her."

"He wanted more than simply to rattle her. He was hoping Sierra would strike him in front of witnesses and be arrested. He wants to separate her from us."

Jason nodded. "It'd be a lot easier to kill her in jail. Or on the way to the police station."

Sierra's complexion grew pale, and she sank into a kitchen chair. "Oliver almost got what he wanted. I pride myself on staying in control, but he triggered me today."

Her tone was stark and self-berating. Unnecessarily so. Oliver had murdered her sister, threatened her life, and attempted to kidnap her nephew. Sierra had shown remarkable strength and resilience through it all. Kyle placed a hand on her shoulder. "You had good reason to be triggered. Believe me, you weren't the only one tempted to punch Oliver."

Jason growled. "To be so close to a murderer and not be able to stop him from driving off was painful."

Addison cast her husband a sympathetic look before picking up the petition. "I'm going to read this over more carefully at home and then prepare a response." She paused. "That is, if you want me to represent you—"

"Absolutely." Sierra rubbed Daniel's back rhythmically. "Thank you for offering, Addy. Of course, I'll pay your rate. I don't expect you to work for free."

"I'd be insulted if you paid me. We're friends now, Sierra. Besides, I owe Kyle a favor or two. He helped Jason save my life when trouble came to my doorstep."

"You don't owe me a thing." Kyle was grateful he'd played a small role in saving Addison from a killer. She was an amazing woman who'd brought Jason a lot of happiness. Since falling in love and getting married, there was a contentment in the former Marine that hadn't been there before. It wasn't an overexaggeration to say that Addison had changed the direction of Jason's life.

Was Sierra changing Kyle's? The thought was thrilling and terrifying in equal measure.

Addison and Jason left. Daniel let out a disgruntled wail and Sierra bobbed and weaved, trying to comfort him. Dark circles shadowed the skin under her eyes. "I don't know what's with him. Daniel's colicky on a good day, but tonight he's unusually fussy."

"Do you want me to take him?" Kyle asked. He didn't know much about comforting babies, but he was willing to give it a go. It looked like a stiff breeze could knock Sierra over. She hadn't been sleeping well and the threats on her life, along with Oliver's latest stunt, were obviously weighing on her. "I promise not to use the Tucker-holding-method."

As he'd hoped, the tension pinching Sierra's features melted into a smile. She laughed. "Poor Tucker. He was really trying. Daniel was working himself into a fit when Tucker picked him up. His method may be unconventional, but it worked." Daniel let out another cry. Sierra bit her lip and switched his position from vertical to horizontal, placing the infant against her body and patting his back. "Right now, I'm feeling just as inadequate. I may get desperate enough to try Tucker's baby hold."

"You're far from inadequate." Gerdie stepped away from the sink and wiped her hands on a dish towel. "You're an excellent guardian, but it's been a trying few days. Why don't I take him for a while? Babies are more sensitive than people realize." She cast Sierra a compassionate look. "He may be picking up on your stress."

Sierra nodded and then hesitated. "You must be exhausted after all the cooking and cleaning you did today."

Gerdie waved a dismissive hand. "Nonsense. I loved every minute." She smiled, the wrinkles around her eyes crinkling, and reached for Daniel. She nestled the baby in her arms. "Now, little one, we're going to sit for a spell in the rocking chair and sing lullabies." She winked at Sierra. "If we're lucky, sleep will come."

She left the kitchen on soft soles slippers, her quiet humming fading as she walked to the living room where the rocker was located next to a window overlooking the backyard. Sierra sank into a chair, crossed her arms over the table, and laid her head in the makeshift cranny. Her silky hair parted like a flowing stream revealing the nape of her neck.

Vulnerable. Weary. Grief-stricken. Kyle wanted to bundle Sierra in thick blankets, tell jokes to make her laugh, and feed her soup to restore the color in her cheeks. It wasn't because she couldn't care for herself. No, Sierra was more than capable and fiercely independent. She also put everyone else before her own needs. Like when his mother offered to take Daniel, Sierra hadn't jumped at the chance to rest. She'd considered his mother's own exhaustion first.

Kyle wanted to give Sierra what she provided for everyone else. She deserved to be cared for and cherished.

He pushed away from the counter and placed a hand on each of Sierra's shoulders. His thumbs gently kneaded the knots of tension from the muscles along the length of her neck. She made a noise of appreciation and raised her head. Her eyes were blurry with exhaustion. "That feels amazing."

Kyle kept massaging her muscles. "It's late. While Mom has Daniel, it's a good time for you to grab some shut-eye."

"I couldn't possibly sleep. I'll just lie in bed, tossing and turning, while my mind works through the problems piling up on my plate." She sighed. "One thing in particular keeps bothering me. I don't understand why Lucy would leave a letter with her attorney explaining to me what's going on, but not provide instructions on how to find the evidence she'd uncovered."

"Maybe there wasn't time."

"No. The letter Lucy wrote to me was dated one day before her death. According to Agent Lewis, that's the same day she called to set up a meeting with him. She was ready to pass over whatever she'd found. Why not leave a copy with the attorney for me? It's clear from Lucy's letter that she understood the risk. My sister was careful and diligent. She backed up everything. *Everything*. It's the reason she was such a good accountant. There have to be multiple copies of the evidence."

Kyle considered her argument. "Let's assume for the sake of this conversation that Lucy made multiple copies, and one of them was for you in case something went awry. She'd want to make sure it didn't fall into enemy hands."

Sierra jolted upright with a gasp. Then she sprung from the chair. Her eyes shone with fresh enthusiasm, erasing her fatigue. "You're a genius."

"Well, I don't know about genius, but I'm..." His voice trailed off as Sierra spun on her heel and headed out of the kitchen on quick strides. "Hey, where are you going?"

Sierra didn't answer. He followed her out of the kitchen, down the hall, and into the office. She punched in the code on the desk safe and it popped open. "Lucy and I were fascinated as kids with treasure hunts and secret messages. We used to take turns creating mysteries for each other to solve. Sometimes our school friends would play along too. One of Lucy's favorite tricks was to leave an obvious clue in a letter, but then hide a more important one by using lemon juice. You dip your finger or a Q-tip into lemon juice and use it to write a message. It dries clear, making it invisible to the naked eye."

Kyle remembered the trick from a science experiment in middle school. Heat was necessary to view the message. He grabbed the desk lamp and flipped it upside down so the bulb was exposed. "Here."

Sierra removed her sister's letter from the envelope and unfolded it. She slowly waved it over the bulb. Letters darkened on the bottom of the paper like magic, revealing an address and then a string of numbers. Sierra grinned. "Oldest trick in the book, but it still works."

"It was smart of her to use a method you would think of. I doubt Oliver would consider waving this letter in front of a light bulb." Kyle set the lamp down. "Do you know the address?"

"No." She frowned, pointing to the string of numbers. "These are the first 16 digits of pi though. Weird. Why would Lucy include that?"

Her tone was distant and the question didn't seem directed at him, so Kyle didn't bother to answer. He sat in the desk chair and wriggled the mouse to activate his laptop. A few keystrokes later and he had the house pulled up on a national real estate website. The property was located within five minutes of a new amusement park on the outskirts of Austin and had recently changed ownership. Kyle pulled up the records and his heart skipped a beat. "The house belongs to Bea James."

Sierra reared back. "Lucy's friend?" She leaned over his shoulder to view the screen. The scent of her lavender perfume filled his senses, and he breathed it in. She flipped through photos on the website before scanning the information. "Looks like Bea's using it as a rental property. I have her phone number. Let's call her."

Kyle pulled out his phone and typed in the digits, putting the call on speaker before handing the device to Sierra. Bea answered on the second ring. She sounded breathless.

"Hi, Bea, it's Sierra. Sorry to call so late, but I have a question. Do you own a house at 164 Maple Street?"

"Sure do. It's an investment property I bought last year. I rent it out to families looking to stay in Austin. Why?"

"Did Lucy ever stay there? Or did she have a key to the house?"

"The house has a keyless entry. Lucy had the code to the front door." Bea paused. "Does this have anything to do with her murder?"

"It might." Sierra started pacing the length of the office. "Is there any way I could come and see the place tomorrow morning? It's important."

"Absolutely." The women arranged a time and then hung up.

Kyle leaned back in his chair. "I don't think you should be the one to go. It's too dangerous. Tucker or Logan can conduct a search and report back."

She shook her head, sending ripples through her dark hair. "I have to go there. I'm sure Lucy left a clue in the house, and it's probably something only I would recognize."

Kyle didn't like it. Leaving the ranch property exposed Sierra to danger, but what other choice was there? She knew her sister better than anyone. They needed to follow the trail Lucy had laid out in the hopes it would lead to Oliver and his thugs locked in a steel cage. He gritted his teeth and nodded. "Okay. We'll head out first thing tomorrow morning."

EIGHTEEN

Sierra slipped on her sunglasses and breathed in the sweet smell of morning dew and pine drifting through the open truck window. The fresh air washed away some of her exhaustion. Discovering the secret message in Lucy's letter provided a new lead to follow, but it didn't eliminate the threats facing her. To make matters worse, Daniel had been fussy and unsettled for most of the night. Sleep had been elusive.

The gun holstered at the small of her back was both foreign and reassuring. Tucker's training had been thorough. Sierra knew how to clean and maintain her weapon as well as shoot it. The former Army Ranger had been patient with a good sense of humor, but never once during their time together did Sierra's heart flutter. She glanced at Kyle in the driver's seat and butterflies alighted in her stomach. His profile was striking, the hard planes softened only by the curve of his cheek and lips. The scent of his aftershave—something spicy and clean—mixed with the fresh air to make an intoxicating fragrance.

She tore her gaze away from Kyle and focused back on the road. Friends. They were just friends. Sierra had been repeating that mantra since the attack in the woods, but her heart refused to listen.

It'd become entangled. Kyle was the type of man she'd always dreamed of. Kind, gentle, brave. The schoolgirl crush she'd developed on him in high school had morphed into something stronger and more powerful.

She was falling in love with him.

There wasn't any chance Kyle would return her feelings. His heart still belonged to his deceased fiancée. Not that it mattered. Sierra's life was nothing short of a mess, and she wasn't in a position to commit to anyone. Her mind understood all the reasons why developing deeper feelings was a terrible idea, but emotion didn't follow in rational channels.

"Last night after you went to bed, I did some research into Jackson Construction," Kyle said, pulling Sierra from her fruitless train of thought. Jackson Construction was the company Lucy believed to be part of Blackstorm. "Ownership is hidden behind several shell corporations. I won't bore you with the details, but I unearthed the wizard behind the curtain."

In other words, he'd hacked into databases to find the real owner. Sierra didn't like the idea, but lives were on the line. Hers and Daniels. Innocent civilians as well, based on the shooting at the cafe. The sooner Oliver was behind bars, the better, and if that meant breaking a few rules along the way...well, she trusted Kyle to maneuver the ethical line with prudence. "Who's the owner?"

"Iris Watson."

Sierra gasped, her mouth dropping open. "My sister's boss." Her mind whirled with the new information. "That doesn't make any sense. Why would Iris ask Lucy to do the accounting for Jackson Construction if she knew the company was involved in something illegal?"

"She didn't." Kyle exited the freeway before turning right. Grocery stores and strip malls lined either side of the road. "I went back through your sister's work files. Lucy was doing the books for Wood Pile. They supply lumber to Jackson Construction. Whatever she saw in her client's books must've made her curious. Since she had access to Jackson Construction's files through the accounting firm, Lucy started digging and stumbled into a hornet's nest."

It sounded just like her sister. Lucy couldn't let a mystery go. They'd often joked that she should've become a detective. Grief swelled inside Sierra and she battled it back, forcing herself to focus on the conversation. "It's surprising Iris didn't restrict access to Jackson Construction's files with a password or something."

"It would've been more secure. Still, Iris must've figured out Lucy was digging around."

Sierra nodded. "She contacted Oliver and..."

Her throat tightened. Lucy was murdered. The words couldn't make it past her constricted airway. She blinked back tears and forced herself to focus on the anger fighting for attention amid the grief. Outrage was fuel that would help her get justice. Sierra took a breath and let it out slowly. "Iris is in this up to her eyeballs."

"So it would seem."

The implications were troubling, especially since, according to the GPS, they were getting close to Bea's house. Kyle turned into a neighborhood. The streets were lined with young trees and cookie-cutter houses painted in various shades of muted browns and blues. Sierra bit her lip. "Do you think Bea can be trusted?"

"Nothing is certain, but her tip about Jackson Construction was spot-on. If she's involved in Blackstorm, why give us that information?"

"True."

Kyle parked at the curb of a one-story home with a tiny front stoop. The siding was cream and matched the garage door. Everything about the property was generic, including the bushes surrounding the single baby tree in the front yard. Bea, standing in the driveway next to her sedan, lifted a hand in greeting.

Sierra responded in kind and then scanned the surrounding area. It was a Saturday morning and the street was lined with cars. Kids played ball in the cul-de-sac and a man was mowing his postage stamp-sized lawn.

Nerves jittered her stomach. They hadn't been followed, which gave her some peace of mind, but her Evan was resourceful. Every minute off the ranch exposed them to potential danger.

Please, God, keep us safe. Give me the ability to recognize the clues Lucy has left and the strength to see this through to the end.

Kyle hopped out of the truck and circled the vehicle to open her door. Together, they walked toward Bea. Sierra greeted her sister's friend and coworker with a smile. "Thanks for doing this."

"No problem. I want to help in any way I can." Bea escorted them to the front porch. She keyed in a code, which unlocked the front door. The hinges creaked as it swung inward. "There aren't any renters this weekend, so feel free to open drawers or look in closets."

Bea stepped back, allowing Sierra and Kyle to enter first. The home had an open floor plan with the living room, kitchen, and dining room visible from the front door. The generic theme from the yard continued indoors. The furnishings were neutral colors and a bit mismatched, as if they'd come from estate or yard sales. Family-friendly games were piled in the cabinet cubby under a large-screen television. Sunlight beamed through the rear windows and a door led to a tiny fenced backyard devoid of flowers. A hallway shot off toward the back of the house.

Sierra didn't have the foggiest notion what she was looking for. She wandered around the main living space, opened all the drawers and cabinets in the kitchen, and looked behind the store-bought pictures on the wall. There was nothing unusual. She kept Bea engaged in conversation during the search, asking about the accounting firm and Lucy. If the woman was involved in Blackstorm, she was an excellent liar. Bea answered her questions without hesitation. It uncoiled the knot of tension in Sierra's stomach. She hated to think Lucy had been betrayed by a close friend.

A tour of the three bedrooms and two bathrooms also turned up nothing of value. Frustrated, Sierra closed the master closet door and headed back into the living room. She walked to the windows overlooking the yard. The grass was brown in patches, but there was no indication anyone had recently dug a hole.

Placing her hands on her hips, Sierra turned. A flash of color caught her eye. Enclosed in a glass-fronted cabinet in the television stand was a statue. It was half-hidden behind several board games. Sierra's heart leapt to her throat. She pointed to the item. "Bea, do you know where that came from?"

"No." Bea tilted her head in thought. "I've never seen it before. It's been months since I've been to the house though. I have a management company that handles the renters and cleaning crew. It's possible someone left it behind."

"Someone did. Lucy." Sierra opened the cabinet and pulled out the statue. It was a mother embracing her little boy in a hug. The painted porcelain was cool to the touch.

"How can you be sure it was Lucy who left it behind?" Kyle asked.

"Because I gave her this statue when she gave birth to Daniel." She'd seen it in a store window and hadn't been able to resist purchasing the item for her sister. It wasn't an accident that Lucy had chosen this particular object. It was a message to Sierra in more ways than one. She could almost hear Lucy whisper, "Take care of my little boy."

As if he sensed the sorrow coursing through her, Kyle eased closer and placed a hand on the small of her back. His presence steadied her. "Since Lucy knew the code to the front door, she must've come by on the day before her death and slipped this into the cabinet. It's another clue."

"Let's hope it's the last one. Is there a way to slip something inside the statue?"

Sierra flipped the object upside down, revealing a hole in the bottom. She stuck a finger inside and felt a hard object tucked along the wall. "There's something in here—"

Glass shattered. Kyle's body collided with Sierra's and they fell to the carpet in a tangle of arms and legs. The air whooshed from her lungs. Thuds in rapid succession punched the wall across from the window and more glass rained down on them. Kyle's arms wrapped around Sierra, pulling her close and tucking her under his hard form.

Someone was shooting at them. Oliver's thugs were here.

The gunshots stopped as abruptly as they started. Sierra's heartbeat roared in her ears, and she shoved against Kyle's chest. There was no time to waste. They needed to get out of the house. "Are you hurt?"

"No. You?"

She took a moment to make an assessment. Her elbow hurt from falling on the carpet and the holstered gun at the small of her back dug into her skin, but other than that, she was unharmed. "I'm okay."

Kyle released her and sucked in a breath. Sierra lifted her head and saw Bea lying on the carpet, blood spreading across the silky fabric of her blouse. Panic spread through her. "No! Bea!"

She crawled to the other woman. There was so much blood. Her sister's friend was alive, eyes opened and fixed on Sierra's face. Both her hands were pressed to the wound on her stomach. Sierra tore off her shirt, leaving only her undershirt on, and pressed the garment to Bea's midsection. "Hang in there. We're going to get you help."

Kyle was already holding the phone to his ear. More glass shattered, this time in the kitchen. A roar followed as flames erupted, seemingly out of nowhere. Smoke started to fill the house.

"Molotov cocktail," Kyle yelled over the din created by the fire. Sparks hit the curtains in the dining room and set them ablaze. The heat was intense. Flames licked their direction, fueled by the fresh air coming in the busted windows, and the smoke thickened.

Sierra coughed, hunkering closer to the floor. "We have to get out of here. The front door is the best way."

Kyle grabbed her arm. "We can't. The house is surrounded. They'll shoot us the moment we show ourselves."

The horror of his words sank into Sierra. Terror made her hands tremble.

They were trapped.

NINETEEN

They were in a desperate situation.

Kyle mentally pictured the layout of the house. The front and back doors were being guarded by men armed and ready to shoot. Windows weren't an option either. Climbing out was too slow. The police were on the way, but they wouldn't make it in time to save them. Smoke was filling the house at a rapid rate as the flames grew more aggressive. They were sitting ducks.

Exactly as Evan planned. Kyle knew Blackstorm's head eliminator had to be responsible for this attack. It was well-planned and coordinated. How had he known they were coming to Bea's house? Was her phone tapped? It was a distinct possibility and one he mentally berated himself for not considering earlier.

"What do we do?" Sierra asked. Her hands pressed against Bea's stomach, stanching the wound that refused to stop bleeding. "There's got to be a way out of this."

"Attic." Bea's voice barely carried above the roar of the flames. She reached out with a bloody hand and grabbed Kyle's shirt. Her grip was surprisingly strong as she fisted the fabric. Her eyes were determined, locked on his face, as she tried to rise from the floor. "Attic."

The energy it took to convey the message sapped the last bit of her strength. Bea's eyes rolled back into her head and she fell back to the carpet, unconscious. Kyle quickly placed his fingers along the column of her neck. She had a pulse. It was weak, but it was there.

"Attic?" Sierra coughed. "What is she talking about?"

Kyle's own throat felt like it was covered in ash. He collected Bea into his arms. "Escape route. Find the access point. Try the hallway, but stay low."

Sierra released her hold on the shirt covering Bea's wounds, grabbed the statue from the carpet, and crawled toward the hallway. Kyle waited until she was out of sight and then lifted Bea against his chest. There was no way to close the distance to the hallway without putting himself in view of the window. As soon as his head popped up, shots rang out. The smoke provided some protection from the sniper, however, and the bullets missed their mark as he sprinted across the living room.

His heart doubled-timed it as he rounded the corner into safety. Sierra had already found the access point to the attic—a hole cut into the ceiling of the hallway—and tugged on the string to reveal a ladder leading upward. Kyle jerked his chin. "Go."

She scrambled up the wooden ladder and disappeared into the space above. Balancing Bea in his arms, Kyle followed. The space was covered in particle board and housed numerous boxes neatly labeled in block lettering. Sunlight drifted in from a window on the far side. Dust motes danced as Kyle set Bea on the ground.

"Stay here," he said to Sierra. Her face was covered in soot, her eyes bright blue against her darkened face. She nodded and immediately began pressing her shirt against Bea's wound again.

Kyle left the women, crawling toward the window to gaze outward. No one was in sight. The drop was significant, but Bea had steered them in the right direction. A thin strip of grass and a fence separated them from the neighbor's yard. On the attic floor, next to the window, lay a metal escape ladder designed to be used in case of a fire.

He quickly unlocked the window and shoved it upward. Fresh air blew across his face, drying the sweat on his brow. Kyle waited half a heartbeat to make sure no one was coming around the side of the house before lifting the ladder. It was designed to deposit someone on the grassy yard, but that wouldn't give them the ability to escape. Oliver's thugs had view of the front and back yards. Instead, Kyle positioned the ladder across the fence. "Sierra, come on."

She appeared next to him, clutching the statue. Her hands were coated in Bea's blood and it'd transferred to the porcelain. Kyle pointed to the neighbor's house. "Drop into their yard and hide behind the fence. I'll be right behind you."

For a moment, their gazes met. His breath hitched. Kyle had the urge to lean forward and press a kiss to her lips.

Underneath them, something crashed and heat flared from the attic opening, reminding him that every second was precious. He pulled his gun from the holster at the small of his back. "Go! I'll cover you."

She tucked the statue inside of her shirt and then scrambled onto the ladder. Kyle wanted to monitor her progress, but it was impossible to do so, and still keep watch on both the left and right sides of the house. Their attackers could spot the ladder at any moment and come racing around the corner. Images of every bad thing that could happen raced through Kyle's mind. He shoved them back. Panic and fear wouldn't serve him. A cold stillness enveloped him, snapping his mind into full focus. It was a feeling he remembered from his war-zone days. Focusing on the mission—getting Sierra and Bea to safety —was the only way forward.

His gaze swept back and forth across the yard. Smoke poured in through the open attic access and started filling the space. It burned his throat. Sweat soaked the back of his shirt.

Finally, Sierra dropped into the neighbor's yard, disappearing behind the fence. Kyle let go of the breath he was holding. Tucking his weapon back into the holster, he crossed over to Bea and lifted her into a fireman's hold. She groaned. A good sign. "Stay with me, Bea. I'm gonna get you out of here."

Blood from her wound coated the back of his neck. Kyle eased onto the ladder, checking to make sure it could take their weight before committing fully. His boots thumped against the metal. It was slow going, Bea's added weight on his shoulders threatening to knock him off-balance. He kept one hand wrapped around her legs while using the other to maneuver the rungs.

A shout came from the front of the house. Kyle's heart stuttered. He turned his head in time to see an unfamiliar man race around the corner of the house. The attacker was dressed in dark clothing that matched the menacing expression on his face. He lifted the gun in his hand and fired.

A high-pitched buzz flew past Kyle's head, close enough it nearly spliced his hair. Another gunshot came from the fence line in response. Sierra. She was leaning over the fence, weapon drawn, a fierce determination etched on her features. The thug shifted his weapon in her direction. Kyle's heart screamed prayers even as he scrambled down the ladder.

More gunshots ripped through the air. The thug shrieked and crashed to the ground, clutching his leg.

Kyle dropped to the ground behind the fence with a thud, holding on to Bea to prevent her from tumbling off his shoulders. His gaze shot to Sierra, sweeping across her slender form. She was whole. Unharmed.

Thank you, God.

Kyle grabbed her hand and started running.

TWENTY

Hours later, safely back at Kyle's ranch, Sierra fingered the small key Lucy had hidden in the statue. Stamped in the metal were the words Knoxville Bank. Years ago, her mother had opened a safe deposit box and completed the required documentation so both her daughters had permission to access it. After her death, Sierra and Lucy kept paying for the box. They'd intended to visit Knoxville and collect the documents inside at some point, but life kept getting in the way. Only one key was issued with the box. Lucy had kept it in her jewelry box at home. Sierra hadn't been able to find it after the accident.

Now she knew why.

The low murmur of Kyle's voice as he talked on the phone drifted across the living room. Daniel was napping in his crib while Gerdie and Rob were running errands with Walker as their bodyguard. Darkness had fallen an hour ago. It'd been the longest day yet, filled with hours of police interrogation. Since returning to the ranch, she'd taken a shower and washed her hair, but her throat was still raw from inhaling smoke. Every muscle in her body ached.

But she was alive.

Once again, Sierra sent up a prayer of thanks to God for

protecting them. She followed that up with a request for Him to watch over Bea. They hadn't had any news of her condition since an ambulance whisked her away.

The soft couch cushions behind Sierra beckoned, and she was tempted to sink into their embrace but resisted. Sleep would have to wait. Kyle was talking to Logan, who'd gone to the hospital to check on Bea's condition. She wouldn't catch a wink of rest without knowing if her sister's friend survived the attack.

Kyle hung up the phone, and Sierra stood. She swallowed past the sudden lump in her throat. "How's Bea?"

"Alive. Logan spoke to her mother and got a complete update on what the doctors are saying. The surgery to remove the bullet in her abdomen went well. Bea's in the ICU now and being monitored closely. The doctors had to remove her spleen, but she's expected to make a full recovery."

Sierra breathed out a sigh of relief. Kyle opened his arms and she eagerly stepped into his embrace. Contentment stole over her. She rested her head against his broad chest and listened to the steady thump of his heart. "I'm glad she's okay." A fresh wave of anger pulsed through her veins. "Bea didn't deserve what happened to her today. She was only trying to help us. My father and Evan don't care who becomes collateral damage. They're cold and heartless. I have to stop them, Kyle."

"We will. I promise you, I'm not stopping until every last one of these criminals is behind bars."

She lifted her face to look into his. "Even if it means risking your life? Today was the second time you nearly died."

He scoffed. "I'm tougher than you think. And I have a great partner by my side." He gently tightened his hold around her waist, drawing her even closer. "You saved my life today, Sierra."

His words warmed her. It'd felt good to be useful in a dangerous situation, but the old fear buried deep in the back of her head flared to life. Sierra played with a button on his shirt. "Can I tell you a secret? My mom forced me to take self-defense courses, even tried to get me to learn to shoot, but I fought her every step of the way. Guns reminded me of what happened with my dad the day he shot my dog, of course, but it goes deeper than that."

She was quiet for a long moment, trying to find the right words to explain what she was feeling. Kyle didn't hurry her. He stood waiting, his arms wrapped securely around her. A port in the storm. Sierra curled her finger around the button on his shirt. "I've been afraid of who I'll become. My father is a criminal. A killer. It's in my DNA, too, and I don't want to be anything like him."

Kyle inhaled sharply. With exquisite tenderness, he placed a finger under her chin and lifted her face until she was staring into his eyes. The chestnut-colored depths were sprinkled with shades of gold and lighter brown. The emotion in his gaze held her captive.

"Listen to me." Kyle's voice was tender but held strong conviction. "You are nothing like your father. Nothing. Everything in you is good and beautiful."

Her breath stalled. No one had ever said anything so wonderful to her. Sierra's heart tumbled as the last brick fell from the wall around her heart. There was no going back. Not when it came to Kyle. Every cell in her body was tuned to him as the moment drew out.

Kyle's gaze dropped to her lips and he edged closer. Sierra met him halfway, their mouths meeting in a soft kiss. A mere brush of their lips, but her pulse quickened so much, she was sure he could feel it. Desire coursed through her veins. Kyle gently tilted her head and deepened the kiss.

The world stopped. Sierra had kissed him before, as a teenager, but this was so much more. So much better. It unlocked every secret wish buried inside her heart. Love. Marriage. Staying forever on the ranch with him, raising Daniel together and having more children. Days full of laughter and love.

Kyle ended the kiss, resting his forehead against hers. They were both breathing fast.

As her pulse settled, doubt crept into the crevices of her thoughts. Was it wise to have kissed him? Sierra wasn't sure where Kyle stood with his feelings. Yes, he cared for her. Obviously, he was attracted to her. But could he ever love her? Would he allow himself to?

Worse, what happened if Sierra died? The threats on her life were real and there was no promise she would survive to see her father put in prison. Kyle had already lost his fiancée tragically. It would be selfish to rip open that old wound again.

She backed out of his embrace, her hand reaching up to touch her lips. The kiss was burned into her cells. "We shouldn't have done that."

His gaze skittered away from hers and a flush crept across his cheeks. "You're right. There's so much going on..."

It should have made Sierra feel better that Kyle agreed with her, but his words stung. She fought back the stupid rush of tears that threatened to steal her breath. Sierra was overly tired and emotionally taxed. All that much more reason to put some separation between them. Her heart was going to be broken no matter what, but it didn't have to be completely shattered.

Kyle's cell phone rang and Sierra jumped as the loud ringtone pierced the stillness of the living room. He crossed the room, scooped it up, and answered. "Stewart." Seconds later, Kyle hung up. He didn't look at her. "That was Jason. He caught Agent Lewis lurking on the back side of the property."

She reared back. "Lurking? Do you mean he was attempting to sneak onto the property?"

"Appears so." His jaw tightened. "Jason's bringing him to the house."

TWENTY-ONE

"My GPS directed me to the back road," Agent Jeff Lewis complained. "I've never been out this way and the country roads are confusing."

Kyle leaned against the island counter, assessing the man sitting at his kitchen table. Jeff's hair was mussed and his clothes mud-stained, consequences of being tackled by Jason in the dark while sneaking around the back of the property. His explanation was reasonable, yet something about it didn't ring true. "What were you doing out of your car?"

"I spotted someone in the woods. Jason, obviously." Jeff glowered at the former Marine. "I should arrest you for attacking a federal agent."

"I didn't *know* you were a federal agent." Jason's glare could have boiled water. His arms were crossed over his chest. Connor was next to his master's side. The German shepherd growled, low and threatening, and bared his canines. The hair on the back of his neck stood up.

Jeff eyed the dog with trepidation. "Does he have to do that?"

"He doesn't like you." Jason touched Connor's head, and the dog settled back on his haunches. He would only attack on command. That didn't mean Connor wouldn't let his feelings be known about a subject though.

Kyle took that into consideration. Connor's instinctive dislike mirrored his own. He'd set aside his initial distrust of Jeff because a background check came back clean, and Chief Garcia had also vouched for the lawman.

Maybe that'd been a mistake.

Connor growled again, as if to remind everyone of his feelings. Kyle shared a look with Jason, sensing there was more to the story. He tilted his head toward the back patio. His friend nodded in silent reply. They excused themselves from the kitchen and stepped outside. The night air was cool and, in the distance, thunder rumbled. Rain was coming.

"I don't believe a word he's saying." Jason pitched his voice low to keep the sound from carrying. His gaze never left the kitchen window, his entire focus on the federal agent inside, still seated at the table. "It wasn't me he saw in the woods, that I can assure you. He was driving down the back road, headlights off, and then got out of his vehicle. His actions weren't in line with someone who was lost."

Kyle rocked back on his heels. "Any idea what he was really doing?"

"No. He didn't have a flashlight or night-vision goggles, so I don't think he was trying to breach the security system. But his behavior was weird. Jeff didn't have his gun drawn when he got out of the vehicle. If he'd seen something suspicious in the woods, then he would've been prepared, especially given the level of threats we're dealing with." Jason stroked Connor's head. "I couldn't search his car, but my guess is, Jeff was about to plant some kind of distraction. A bomb, maybe? Something to draw most of us out to the far end of the property, and then, while we were dealing with that, he would be in the house."

Kyle picked up on his friend's train of thought. "Jeff would be in the perfect position to kill Sierra and kidnap Daniel." His gut tightened. Could his friend be right? It was a terrifying prospect. "I wonder if that's the real reason Oliver showed up here the other day. Maybe he was hoping we'd let him inside and then his hitmen could create chaos on the outskirts of the property dividing us."

Jason nodded, his mouth pressed into a thin line. "It's worth consideration. There isn't much evidence to support that theory, but it's the most logical one based on what we know. I'd be careful about what you share with Mr. FBI agent. He may be clean on paper, but that doesn't mean he can be trusted."

"Understood." Kyle considered his options. "Stay within visual range out here. I have to speak to Sierra in private and explain the situation. I don't want to leave Jeff alone in the kitchen, but I also don't want him to know he's being watched."

"You got it."

Kyle clapped his friend on the shoulder before heading back inside the kitchen. "Okay, I explained to Jason that you're here to help." Years of military training kept his stance casual and his tone easy. He didn't want Jeff to realize they suspected him of lying. "He's protective of Sierra. As we all are."

Jeff's expression was sour, as if he'd been sucking on a bucket of lemons. He'd been typing something on his phone but stopped the moment Kyle opened the back door and clicked the device closed. He dropped the phone to the table and it landed with a clatter. "I need to speak to Sierra. Where is she?"

His words were clipped, the arrogance he couldn't hide edging back to the surface. Kyle bristled inwardly but plastered a friendly smile on his face. "I'll get her."

He slipped from the kitchen. Kyle paused at the entrance of the hall, gathering his emotional walls in preparation to see Sierra. The kiss they'd shared earlier in the evening was imprinted on his brain. He could no longer deny the depth of his feelings, but facing them didn't bring answers. He was stepping into unknown territory and the last thing he wanted was to hurt Sierra. Could he commit to someone new? Was he ready to risk his heart?

He wasn't sure. Kyle had made promises to Maisy. He'd vowed to love her forever and didn't know how to reconcile that pledge with his feelings for Sierra. It was a confusing mess. And not one that he could focus on right now. Keeping Sierra and Daniel safe was the priority. Everything else would have to wait.

Kyle let out a breath and stepped into the hallway. Sierra was just coming out of the bedroom she shared with Daniel. The infant was wrapped in a footed onesie. Trucks marched across the fabric. He was whimpering, his tiny face red, hands balled into fists. Worry creased Sierra's brow, and she was nibbling on her lower lip. Concern shot through Kyle. "What's wrong?"

"He has a cold." Sierra ran a hand over the baby's downy hair, smoothing it. "Your mom called the pediatrician in town and we spoke to him. He doesn't think there's anything to worry about since Daniel isn't running a fever, but we should monitor him closely." She glanced toward the kitchen. "What's going on with Jeff?"

Kyle hated to add more worries to her plate, but there was no way to avoid it. He quickly explained the situation. "I don't think we should tell him about the safe deposit box key. Not yet. First thing Monday morning, we go to the bank and retrieve the evidence. I'll make copies and we can distribute them to Chief Garcia and Jeff at the same time."

"That sounds like a good plan." Sierra squared her shoulders. "Let's go see what Jeff has to say. I have to feed Daniel anyway."

They went into the kitchen. Kyle offered to hold the baby while Sierra made his bottle. Despite his aunt's best intentions, the baby's hair was too fine to lie close to his head. It swirled in the air wildly, giving Daniel the faint appearance of having stuck his finger in a light socket. His sweet blue eyes shimmered with tears and his nose was running. Kyle gently wiped it with a tissue from the counter, a tenderness unlike any other sweeping over him. Sierra wasn't the only one who'd slipped past Kyle's defenses. He would do anything for this child.

Jeff's gaze was like a laser on Kyle's skin. He met the other man's eyes and caught a flicker of something akin to hatred in their depths. It disappeared so quickly, Kyle second-guessed whether he'd seen it there in the first place. Were his suspicions of the lawman getting the best of him?

Sierra shook the baby's bottle to mix the formula and joined them at the table, taking Daniel back into her arms. Once the baby was settled, she turned to Jeff. "What did you need to talk to me about?"

"We've officially tied Jackson Construction and Iris Watson to Blackstorm." Jeff frowned. "Unfortunately, she's missing. Iris never showed up to work yesterday and none of her neighbors have seen her in the last forty-eight hours. We've alerted every law enforcement agency in the country to be on the lookout for her. I hope she'll be in custody soon."

"That's good news." Sierra arched a brow. "But I have a feeling there's some bad news to go with it."

"You'd be right. George Sampson, the sniper from the cafe, hasn't agreed to say very much, but he claims we have it all wrong. Oliver isn't the leader of Blackstorm."

"That's impossible." The words were spoken softly to avoid disturbing Daniel, but they had all the force of a bullet. "George is lying. My father was arrested and tried for murder. He's been under investigation by authorities for decades."

"And no evidence has ever conclusively linked him to Blackstorm. We have to consider George is telling the truth. The investigation is far from over, but Iris could be the leader of the organization."

Sierra's mouth popped open to argue and then shut again. Shock leached the blood from her face. Kyle placed a hand on her knee under the table, turning his attention to Jeff. "If that's true, then why come after Sierra? It's clear the attacks were designed to kill her and kidnap Daniel. Oliver is the only one with motive to want both those things."

"Not necessarily. The leader of Blackstorm wants Sierra dead to prevent her from finding the evidence Lucy uncovered. Kidnapping Daniel may be a ruse to throw us off the trail and have authorities continue to investigate Oliver."

Kyle wanted to argue with Jeff, but even he had to agree that the theory was a possibility. Frustration tore at him. Everything they knew about the threats against Sierra was built on quicksand. There were few solid facts. Except one.

Whoever was behind these attacks wanted Sierra dead.

TWENTY-TWO

Was Iris the leader of Blackstorm?

Sierra rolled over in bed. She'd tossed and turned most of the night, her mind jumping from one problem to the next. Daniel's cold. The threats. George's claims. Her feelings for Kyle. The thoughts rattled inside her brain on endless loops, frustration building as the hours crept by. Prayer had helped her settle into sleep, but the issues roared back to the surface the moment she opened her eyes.

Rain pattered against the window. It'd stormed all night, the thunder loud enough to rattle the house windows. Sierra tossed off the covers, reaching for her phone. She jolted. It was nearly nine in the morning. Daniel should have woken her thirty minutes ago for his feeding.

She flew across the room to his crib. The baby was sleeping, but there was a flush to his cheeks. Sierra touched his skin and it was warm to the touch. Suspecting a fever, she retrieved the ear thermometer Gerdie had provided. Daniel fussed as she used the device, his stuffy nose weakening his cries. Sierra had been sucking the mucus out with a suction bulb, as directed by the doctor, and regularly checking the baby for a fever. There hadn't been any cause for additional concern.

Until this morning. The thermometer beeped. Sierra's heart sank when she saw the number on the screen. Daniel had a fever. It was low grade, but it was there. She scooped him into her arms and placed a kiss on his forehead to soothe his whimpering cries. "I know, sweetie. You don't feel good."

Sierra tried to rationalize away the thread of panic rising in her. Babies got colds and fevers all the time, didn't they? She'd read numerous baby books and talked to other moms online before the threats on her life had taken over. Sickness was a normal part of childhood. Daniel would be fine, but she'd feel a lot better once he saw a doctor.

She quickly dressed, then changed Daniel's diaper and cleared his nose, before going into the kitchen. The scent of fresh coffee greeted her. Kyle sat at the kitchen table, a mug at his elbow, typing on a laptop. He glanced up as she entered the room. Her distress over Daniel's condition must've been obvious, because he immediately rose. "What's wrong?"

"He has a fever. The pediatrician mentioned yesterday that there's an urgent care clinic in town that's open 24/7. Do you know where it is? Daniel needs to see a doctor. I want to make sure we're still dealing with a simple cold and not something more serious."

"Of course. I know where the clinic is." Kyle checked his watch. "My parents and the guys went to church this morning. They won't be back for a few hours."

The arrangements to attend church had been made last night. Sierra and Kyle opted to skip the service since the ranch security system had kept them safe. Taking Daniel off the property to see the doctor was risky, but there wasn't a choice. The pediatrician had been clear in his instructions. If the infant developed a fever, she needed to have him examined.

"I don't think we can wait." Sierra knew it was silly to be so concerned, but Daniel was just a baby. He couldn't tell her how he was feeling. There was a danger of pneumonia or RSV. Both were serious, and if treatment was delayed, Daniel could end up in the hospital.

Kyle grabbed his keys from a nearby rack. "Come on. Let's get him to the doctor."

Sierra scooped up the diaper bag from the bench by the door, and moments later, they were heading toward town. Daniel ate very little of his bottle along the way, sending Sierra's worry into the stratosphere. She sighed with relief when they entered the emergency clinic's parking lot.

Kyle circled the truck and opened her door. "Here, let me take Daniel."

She handed the baby over before hitching the diaper bag to her shoulder. Kyle scanned the parking lot, his muscles tense, as he hurried them through the drizzle to the entrance. His constant vigilance was reassuring, but it was also a reminder of the danger hovering in the background.

The doctor inside the clinic was thorough and kind. He shared Sierra's concern about the fever and praised her for bringing the baby in but assured her Daniel only had a cold. "Offer him plenty of formula to keep him hydrated. You can purchase a humidifier from the pharmacy to keep the air moist as well. To lower his fever, give him a bit of infant Tylenol." The doctor smiled at Sierra. "You're doing a great job managing things thus far. If things get worse, or if you have any other concerns, bring him back in."

The tension in her muscles released and Sierra's spine relaxed as the doctor left the room. "Whew. What a relief." She kissed Daniel's plump hand before turning to Kyle. "Thanks for supporting my decision to bring him right in. Maybe I overreacted—"

"No you didn't." Kyle handed her Daniel's outfit, which had to be removed for the exam. "The doctor even said as much. Babies are tricky because they seem fine and then take a turn for the worse quickly." He ran a hand over Daniel's wild hair, a soft smile on his face. "I'm just glad the little man is okay."

Sierra's heart skittered. Kyle was so gentle and caring with Daniel. He'd make an outstanding father, and his actions today only cemented the thought. Before she could stop herself, Sierra leaned her head on Kyle's arm. No matter how much she reasoned with her heart, it refused to listen.

He wrapped his arm around her in a side hug and then kissed the top of her head. "There's a pharmacy next door. We can run over and grab the Tylenol and humidifier before heading back to the ranch."

"That would be great."

He caught and held her gaze. As if by a magnetic pull, their lips found each other. The kiss was tender and sweet, a quick caress that belied the ocean of emotions underneath. Kyle pulled back and his lips quirked up. "We can't stop kissing each other."

A laugh burst from Sierra. "No, we can't."

It brought up a thousand questions, but now wasn't the time to get into them. Besides, she wanted to hang on to this moment of happiness for as long as possible. Sierra finished dressing Daniel before using the quiet exam room to feed him more formula. He took the bottle much better than in the car.

The weather was gloomy as they traversed the covered walkway to the pharmacy. Dark thunder clouds hovered in the distance promising more storms to come. Sierra shivered and wrapped the blanket tighter around the baby. The hair on the back of her neck stood on end. She glanced over her shoulder but didn't see anyone in the parking lot. Still, the feeling of being watched crept over her.

"What is it?" Kyle asked, his gaze sweeping the surrounding area.

"Maybe nothing. I'm a bit jumpy."

They picked up the pace. A friendly store clerk assisted them in finding the right items and rang them up. Daniel fussed and Sierra swayed with him. Suddenly, the baby made a face and a loud noise emanated from the bottom half of his body. Liquid seeped from his diaper. Sierra's mouth dropped open. He'd had blowouts before, but this one was epic. "Uh, we have a problem."

Kyle glanced at her, bag in hand, and his eyes widened. "Holy smokes."

"Where's your bathroom?" Sierra asked the store clerk.

He pointed to the rear of the store, and she hurried down the aisle, the diaper bag hitting against her hip. Kyle followed. "Can I do something to help?"

It was a sweet offer, but he couldn't follow her into the restroom since the pharmacy didn't have a family-designated one. The dampness had seeped into her shirt. Sierra turned to face him, her back to the ladies' room. "Give me five minutes."

"Sure thing. I'll be waiting right here."

She jerked her chin toward the sack in his hand. "Tuck the medication into the pocket of the diaper bag. Daniel needs some now anyway."

Kyle did as she asked and Sierra ducked into the bathroom. It was clean and equipped with a baby-changing station. She sang a song to Daniel while using half a box of wipes to clean him. He blinked at her antics, the hint of a smile playing on his lips. Sierra's heart swelled with happiness and love. She quickly redressed him in a clean outfit, tackled her own stained clothing, and measured out the medication he needed. Daniel swallowed it without complaint.

The door to the bathroom creaked open and an elderly woman entered, leaning heavily on a cane. The changing station when lowered blocked access to the stall. Sierra barely glanced up as she zipped the diaper bag closed. "I'm all done. Let me get out of your way."

The woman rushed her, lifting the cane and whacking Sierra in the back of the head with the hard iron handle. Stars exploded across her vision. She reached for the gun holstered at her waist but wasn't fast enough. Sierra cried out as Daniel was ripped from her arms. The force of the struggle sent her pinwheeling back. She landed on the bathroom floor hard, pain shooting up her tailbone. She barely felt it. For a brief second, Sierra and the woman were face-to-face. Recognition zipped through her.

Iris.

Daniel sent up a howling cry as the attacker whirled on her heels and sped for the exit. Sierra scrambled to her feet, screaming. "No!"

She raced for the door, panic fueling her steps, and then went sprawling as she tripped over something in the aisle. Carpet burned the soft parts of her hands as she instinctively flung out her arms to brace herself against the fall. Her foot was tangled with something and wouldn't come free. Sierra whirled.

Kyle. He was unconscious on the ground. A deep red mark covered his throat. Dead? Horror snaked through her, increasing her screams. Her sneaker was hooked on his belt. In the corner of the aisle, the store clerk held his chest, panting. His face was ashen, lips bloodless. A spilled bottle of medication was scattered on the floor. Her brain couldn't make sense of the scene.

A squeal of tires outside ripped through her shock. Daniel. Sierra bolted to her feet and raced for the exit of the pharmacy. A blast of cold air and rain smacked her in the face. An SUV, Evan at the wheel, rounded the corner of the building and flew out of the parking lot.

Sierra screamed for help, but it was no use.

Daniel was gone.

TWENTY-THREE

The pounding in his head wouldn't abate, but it was nothing compared to the ache in his heart.

Kyle leaned against the wall, watching Sierra across the room as she stared out the window. Her hair was damp and uncombed. Scrapes marred the visible skin along her hands and above the collar of her shirt.

It'd been an hour since Daniel was kidnapped. Chief Garcia had taken their initial statements at the pharmacy and then advised Kyle to bring Sierra back to the ranch for her own safety. She'd protested, wanting to stay and aid in the search for Daniel, but the chief refused. Her presence put everyone around her at risk. The officers and potentially innocent civilians.

Blackstorm's leader still wanted her dead, after all.

Sierra hadn't spoken a word since leaving the pharmacy. No tears glittered on her cheeks and her expression was stark. One hand clutched the cross dangling from her necklace. It wasn't shock. It was grief. A crippling pain so bone deep it couldn't be put into words. Kyle didn't need her to explain it. He shared the feeling.

Muffled footsteps came from the office. Nathan appeared at

Kyle's side. His expression was grim, mouth drawn into a hard line. "Tucker called. The guys and your parents have volunteered to join the search effort. Chief Garcia has called in the FBI and state police. Daniel's photograph and details about the kidnapping are already playing on the news, along with a monetary tip to anyone who provides information that aids in the baby's recovery. He's not wasting a moment."

"I knew he wouldn't." Chief Garcia was a good man and an excellent law enforcement officer. Last year, Cassie, Nathan's wife, had a stalker. The chief had been attacked by the man and nearly killed while investigating. He wouldn't stop until Daniel was found, even if that meant searching every nook and cranny of Texas.

Kyle's hands balled into fists. "I messed up, Nate. Iris and Evan walked right into the pharmacy and I didn't recognize them."

His cousin's tone was sympathetic. "The news report said they were wearing disguises."

They had been. Iris was dressed as an elderly woman in baggy clothes, a gray wig, and a cane. She'd come into the pharmacy on her "son's" arm. Evan had grown a beard and put a ball cap over his head. Kyle should've recognized him, even with the minor changes, but Iris's disguise threw him off. He hadn't anticipated them being together.

"I don't know if they planned to attack us in the pharmacy from the beginning, or they were simply following us, waiting for an opportunity." Kyle had replayed the chain of events in his mind a thousand times since the kidnapping. It wasn't helping, but he couldn't stop. "The store clerk started gasping and holding his chest. I realized he was having a heart attack. Grabbed some aspirin, helped him swallow it. Evan took advantage of the distraction and snuck up behind me. He put me in a choke hold." The memory of the attack swept through him. Kyle had been in dangerous and deadly situations before, but this...this was different. He'd never felt so powerless. "I couldn't yell to alert Sierra, and because of my position on the ground, I couldn't get leverage to break Evan's hold."

He'd passed out. Chokeholds were quick, effective, and silent. It'd been brilliant to use that particular method to subdue Kyle. The sound of gunshots would've carried and the urgent care clinic next door had security guards.

Mistakes. Mistakes. Mistakes. He should've been more careful, more aware. He'd failed and Sierra paid the price for it. Kyle had woken up on the pharmacy floor with Sierra hovering over him and the wail of police sirens drawing closer. But it was too late. Daniel was gone.

Nathan clapped a hand on his shoulder. "This isn't your fault, cuz. Tucker said the store clerk survived because of your quick actions. Evan and Iris are the only ones to blame." He dropped his hand. "No one is going to stop until Daniel is home safe and sound. In the meantime, Sierra needs you to comfort her. She needs your strength."

He'd been debating crossing the room to speak to her since their arrival at the ranch, but the last thing Kyle wanted was to make things worse. "It wouldn't surprise me if she hates me."

Nathan shook his head. "Not a chance. That woman is in love with you."

Kyle stiffened and turned to face his cousin. Nathan met his gaze straight on, brows lifted. "You're in love with her, too, I reckon. Just too stubborn and pigheaded to admit it."

"I..." He was at a loss for words. Love? Was he in love with Sierra?

"You've been holding on to Maisy's memory so tightly, no woman could ever get close to your heart," Nathan continued. "Until Sierra. God knew what he was doing when he brought the two of you together. You need each other."

Nathan's words struck a chord somewhere deep inside Kyle. His cousin was right. They needed each other, and not just to escape the danger. Sierra and Daniel had reminded him of who he used to be, before the war and Maisy's death. They brought him joy and quiet moments of happiness.

Kyle rubbed his chest. His heart ached, as though it was being torn in two. "I made a promise to Maisy. I swore to love her forever."

Nathan frowned. "I never told you this, but a few months after I came to live here, Aunt Gerdie sat me down. I'd been disrespectful to my teachers, skipping school, and causing trouble."

Kyle remembered that time. Nathan's mom had passed away from cancer and he was struggling to deal with the grief.

"It took some talking, but long story short, I was feeling at home with you guys," Nathan continued. "I loved the ranch and the horses. Family dinners. The whole thing. But it felt like a betrayal to my mom. I had it in my head that loving her meant I couldn't love anyone else. But Aunt Gerdie set me straight. She explained God encourages us to love. It's our greatest gift to others."

That sounded like his mom. Her favorite bible verse was from First Corinthians. "And now these three remain: Faith, hope, and love. But the greatest of these is love."

Nathan nodded. "You can love Maisy forever and appreciate the wonderful time you had together, but that doesn't stop you from loving Sierra and Daniel too. It's not a betrayal." He tilted his head toward the living room. "Go comfort her, Kyle."

He pushed off the wall and straightened his shoulders. Kyle couldn't process everything his cousin had said, but Nathan was right. Sierra was hurting and he didn't want her to do it alone. Not if he could ease her pain in any measure.

On silent steps, he went into the living room. Still, Sierra must've sensed him behind her because she turned and buried her face in his chest. He embraced her. Sierra clung to Kyle as though he was the only thing keeping her standing. Maybe he was. He tightened his arms around her. "We'll get him back."

She fisted the fabric of his shirt. "He's my life, Kyle. I spent the first thirty minutes since his kidnapping worrying about every possibility. Was he cold? Did they have the right formula to give him? But I can't control any of that. I have to trust God to take care of Daniel."

Sierra lifted her face to look into his. "Once I did that, I could think clearly. For the last thirty minutes, I've been forming a plan." Determination flared in her eyes, darkening the color from sky blue to a stormy cobalt. "I have something the leader of Blackstorm wants more than Daniel."

"The evidence."

"We offer them a trade. The evidence for Daniel." She pulled out of Kyle's embrace and then narrowed her gaze. "You've already thought of it."

"I've been playing with the idea. Trouble is, without knowing who the leader of Blackstorm is, we can't be sure what we're dealing with. Iris and Evan could've killed us both today. They didn't. The main goal was to kidnap Daniel, which indicates that your father is behind these attacks."

"Agreed."

"And yet, George told the FBI that Oliver isn't the leader of Blackstorm. What would he have to gain from lying about that?"

Sierra crossed her arms over her chest. "People lie for all kinds of reasons. He could be bored for all we know. Or trying to get investigators to chase their tails. The rumored links between my father and Blackstorm have been around for decades. I don't think they materialized out of thin air." Her expression darkened. "I know Oliver. I know what he's capable of. If he's not the leader of Blackstorm, then he's involved somehow."

"I don't disagree with that statement. Still, I feel like we're trying to put together a puzzle with only half the pieces." Kyle frowned. "Offering to exchange the evidence for Daniel could backfire. We could lose everything, Sierra. The ability to save Daniel and shut down Blackstorm forever. The more prudent decision could be to wait until tomorrow morning, and when the bank opens, we grab the evidence from the safe deposit box and turn it over to the authorities."

She bit her lip and her gaze went back to the window. Silence enveloped them as Sierra mulled over what he'd said. Finally, she shook her head. "I can't risk Daniel's life on what I don't know. There's no guarantee the evidence Lucy collected will be enough to bring Blackstorm down. Or that the FBI can be trusted. My father was on trial for murder until last week and managed to convince a jury he was innocent." She turned to face him. "We need to arrange a trade and get Daniel back."

"And then?"

"He and I have to disappear."

TWENTY-FOUR

Sierra eyed the cell phone on the coffee table. If her plan worked, someone from Blackstorm would call any minute. Kyle sat in the armchair, hands crossed over his lap, the epitome of calm. But she sensed the tension bubbling beneath his cool exterior. Kyle was just better at hiding it than she was. Military training, no doubt.

Outside, lightning flashed. Sierra jumped. Ms. Whiskers howled and skittered into the hidey-hole on the top of her cat stand. She didn't like the storm.

Sierra crossed the room and murmured sweet words to the tabby. She took a chance and dangled her fingers outside the hole. Ms. Whiskers extended a paw, placing it in Sierra's palm. She gently rubbed the cat's toes to comfort her. Anything to take her mind off the phone, quietly mocking her from the coffee table.

The front door opened and a blast of cold air preceded Nathan inside. He was followed by the entire gang. Tucker, Walker, and Logan shook rain off their jackets and hung them by the door before removing their shoes. Jason and Connor were the last of the group to enter. After having his paws cleaned, the German shepherd beelined for Sierra. She stroked his head. "Hey, boy."

Kyle came to stand next to Sierra. He placed a hand on her back in a comforting gesture before greeting his friends. "There's fresh coffee in the kitchen. Grab some if you want and then come into the living room to get an update on what's going on."

The next few minutes were a flurry of activity. Sierra refused offers of both coffee and food. It was a miracle worry hadn't eaten a hole through her stomach lining. Daniel had been kidnapped three hours ago, and every moment away from him felt like torture. It was difficult to breathe. Again and again, she had to remind herself that God was watching over Daniel. He would keep him safe. She had to trust and have faith.

But that didn't mean it was easy.

Once everyone was settled in the living room, Kyle gave a brief rundown of their earlier conversation. The men's faces showed a myriad of emotions. Anger, frustration, worry. But not one of them attempted to talk Sierra out of the plan to trade the evidence for Daniel. She was grateful for that. There was no time to spare, and she didn't have the energy for arguing anyway.

Jason stroked Connor's head. "How did you get in contact with Blackstorm to let them know that you'd located the evidence?"

"I called my father's family law attorney." Sierra picked up the custody papers her father had delivered a few days ago. "His number is on the last page. I told the attorney to call Oliver immediately and say that I'm prepared to make a trade." She set the papers down and gestured to the phone on the coffee table. "I gave him the number to this burner phone."

Tucker leaned forward. "What if Oliver isn't the leader of Blackstorm?"

"I don't think it matters. He's involved somehow. Oliver will call." She crossed her arms over her chest. "Or someone from Blackstorm will. They won't risk the evidence ending up in the hands of law enforcement."

"Hold on." Logan's dark hair was damp from the rain and sticking up in wild spikes as if he'd run his hand through it a thousand times. "I hate to point out the flaw in this plan, but we don't actually have the evidence Lucy stole. We *think* it's in the safe deposit box. What if it's not?"

She hadn't considered that. The key was looped around a chain on her neck, next to the cross. "It has to be there. The safe deposit box is the best place for Lucy to have hidden the evidence."

"The trade-off should happen at the bank." Tucker stroked his beard. "Lots of cameras and security. The Knoxville Police Department can surround the building with SWAT and keep it clear of civilians to lower the risk. Plain clothes officers can even pose as bank tellers."

Nathan frowned. "Criminals can spot cops from a mile away, even out of uniform. Oliver, if he calls, won't allow us a chance to have the police or the FBI there."

"The same thought occurred to me," Kyle said. "I've already called Chief Garcia. Apparently, Knoxville City Council has granted the police chief the right to deputize private citizens if necessary. He's agreed to deputize us so we can be inside the bank alongside undercover officers who are used to fitting in with criminals without being detected. SWAT will be stationed a mile away from the bank, waiting. Oliver won't think anything about seeing us inside the bank since we've been protecting Sierra all this time. In fact, I guarantee he'll be expecting it."

He leaned forward. "Of course, I don't expect any of you to put your lives on the line. This mission is risky—"

Nathan tossed his hands dismissively. "We've faced worse."

The other men made similar remarks. Some light teasing and jabs were thrown in for good measure as they ribbed each other about their levels of service and times of deployment. Walker and Logan started wrestling. Despite the seriousness of the situation, Sierra smiled. She'd grown fond of the guys and their rough-and-tumble ways. It was clear how much they all cared about each other. And Kyle.

Kyle whistled to bring the attention back to the matter at hand. Once everyone had settled back down, he continued, "Nothing can be put in motion, however, unless Blackstorm calls. If we play it right, Oliver will show up personally to make the trade-off. He'll be arrested, Daniel will be safe and sound, and the evidence Lucy hid will end up with the right authorities."

A shadow darkened his expression as he glanced toward Sierra. Their gazes caught and held. A thousand unsaid words seemed to pass between them, and she bit her lip to hold back a wave of tears. She didn't want to do this. Any of it. But there was no choice.

"The FBI will take the evidence and use it to bring Blackstorm down," Kyle continued. "But that'll take time and Sierra is worried her father will be free to exact revenge. We need to make an escape plan for her and Daniel."

Nathan reared back. "What kind of escape plan?"

"I need to disappear," she said. "Completely. Daniel and I will need new IDs, social security numbers, the whole works."

This time a round of objections followed from Kyle's friends. She raised a hand to interrupt them. "It's not my favorite choice either, but keeping Daniel safe is the most important thing. Escaping with new names protected my mother, Lucy, and me for decades."

Nathan's gaze swung toward his cousin. "You're on board with this?"

"I support Sierra's decision one thousand percent. She's doing what she needs to." Once again, Kyle met her gaze. His brown eyes were tortured. Haunted. This was breaking his heart just as much as it was breaking hers. "I understand that."

This time, she couldn't stop the flood of tears entirely. Sierra swiped at her eyes and sucked in a deep breath to steady her emotions.

Kyle shifted his attention to Walker. "You once mentioned your buddy Travis occasionally helps people disappear, right?"

"Yeah." Walker gripped his coffee mug so tightly his knuckles were white. He cast Sierra a look filled with a mixture of sympathy and frustration. "It's not something his firm, Justice Investigations, advertises, but Travis has helped victims of domestic violence or women being stalked change their names. I'll call him and get the identities fast-tracked."

"Thank you, Walker." Sierra breathed out, relief loosening some of the tension in her muscles. There was a plan. Her attention once again shot to the phone on the coffee table. She willed it to ring.

As if in response to her thoughts, it trilled. The screen lit up and the caller ID read Unknown Number.

Sierra picked it up with a shaking hand. She closed her eyes for a brief second and said a silent prayer before opening them up again. Kyle nodded reassuringly. His presence was steading, and Sierra drew from the strength in his gaze. She could do this. She would do this.

Sierra answered, putting the call on speaker so everyone in the room could hear the conversation. "It's about time you called. I was beginning to think you hadn't gotten my message."

Laughter spilled from the speakers. Cold and hard. "Don't try to act tough. We both know you aren't."

Evan. Of course. Oliver didn't like to get his hands dirty if he could avoid it. She gripped the cell phone in her hand. "Is Daniel okay? He has a cold and needs medication to keep his fever down."

"The baby's fine. He's being taken care of."

His tone had lost that cutting edge, and Sierra hoped he was telling her the truth. "I have the evidence Lucy was going to hand to the FBI. In exchange for handing it over to you instead, I want Daniel back. We can make the trade tomorrow morning at the Knoxville Bank."

"The bank isn't going to work—"

"Too bad. The evidence is locked in a safe deposit box. I'm the only one with permission to access that box and the key to do so. The trade-off happens tomorrow when the bank opens at 8:00 a.m. Daniel needs to be inside the lobby or I'll refuse to hand anything over."

"You really expect me to take orders from you?"

Sierra ignored his insult. She controlled this conversation, not him. "I believe you like your freedom. Prison has bars, Evan, and they don't let the inmates wear designer suits." She let that barb sink in before continuing, "Besides, I've witnessed firsthand how cold and cruel my father can be when you don't do what he wants. Blackstorm will go down if I hand this evidence over to the authorities. The decision is yours. Meet me at the bank with Daniel tomorrow morning or be prepared to run from every lawman *and* my father for the rest of your life."

He was silent. Sierra held her breath, leaning into the phone. All the men in the living room did the same. It was so quiet, she could hear Connor's inhales and exhales.

"Fine," Evan bit out at last. "Tomorrow morning at the bank. But I'm warning you. Don't call the Knoxville Police or the FBI. We have eyes and ears in both departments. If I catch wind that this is a setup, I'll kill you myself."

He hung up. Sierra let out the breath she was holding. It took effort to release her fingers from their iron grip around the phone. "We have a plan, gentlemen. Let's get busy."

TWENTY-FIVE

The next morning brought a break in the thunderstorms. Sunshine poked through the lingering clouds as Kyle steered his truck to the side of the road. The center of town, and Knoxville Bank, were visible through the windshield. They'd left the ranch early, and he didn't want to sit in the bank parking lot until the meeting time. Besides, there was a last-minute detail to take care of.

The stitches along his stomach burned. Phantom pains, since the wound was healing well, but they drew attention to the fear crimping his stomach. Kyle was used to dangerous missions, but this was very different.

He glanced at Sierra out of the corner of his eye. Her dark hair was pulled back, but a few strands had come free and were playing with the delicate curve of her cheek. Scrapes from yesterday's attack still marred her palms. Kyle parked the truck and killed the engine before taking one of her hands in his. He ran his thumb over the wounds.

Yes, this mission differed from any other. This time, he stood to lose everything.

Sierra released her seat belt and leaned across the center console.

She cupped the back of his neck and gently tugged him down for a kiss. It was tender and sweet and filled with heartache. Kyle didn't want to let her go.

He rested his forehead against hers. "I have something for you." He reluctantly released her to reach into the side pocket and retrieve the device he'd placed there for safekeeping. "It's a GPS tracker. Lift the insole of your tennis shoe and slip it underneath."

He placed the small round object in her palm. Sierra quickly placed it in her shoe and Kyle used an app on his phone to make sure it was working. "Tucker and Jason also have the information on your device, so multiple people can track you."

In case something went wrong. Kyle didn't say it, but Sierra was smart enough to figure out the implication on her own. She placed a hand on his arm. "There's something I need to say before we go inside."

"Sierra..." He didn't know if his heart could take this.

"Please, Kyle. Even if everything goes right in there, Daniel and I will immediately be whisked out of state by Walker's friend. This may be the last time we're alone, and I can't leave without saying how I feel." She lifted her gaze to meet his. "I love you. I don't expect you to say it back or feel the same way. I know your heart belongs to Maisy, but—"

He placed a finger gently against her soft lips. His pulse beat a rapid tempo as the truth of what he'd been feeling came crashing over him. "I love you too."

She inhaled sharply, her gaze searching his face. Questions were written in the depths of her gorgeous eyes. Kyle caressed her bottom lip with the edge of his finger. "A part of me will always love Maisy. I won't deny that. But when I think of my future, it's you and Daniel I picture." A smile lifted the corners of his mouth. "I tried fighting these feelings for you, Sierra, but it's impossible. I love you. And Daniel too."

Tears shimmered in her eyes. Kyle kissed her again and the world around them faded away for a moment as he became lost in a sea of emotion. Nathan had been right. God knew what he was doing when Sierra and Daniel dropped into his life. He prayed that what happened next wouldn't tear them apart.

Kyle once again reluctantly released Sierra after brushing her lips with his one last time. She offered him a smile before glancing at the bank visible beyond the windshield. Her expression morphed into one of determination and strength. A warrior's attitude. It fascinated him. Sierra had always been brave, but the last few days had given her a quiet confidence. "You've changed."

"I have." She jutted up her chin. "I know who I am now. And you were a part of that." Sierra took his hands in hers. "It's getting close to eight. Will you lead us in prayer?"

Kyle bent his head. "Lord God, we ask for Your protection. Provide us with the wisdom to make the right decisions and the strength to carry them out. May our actions today serve You by bringing justice to those who've hurt innocent people. In Your name we pray. Amen."

"Amen." Sierra squeezed his hands once before letting go. She snapped her seat belt back on. "Let's go."

Kyle restarted his truck and edged back onto the road. Moments later, they were pulling into the bank parking lot. There was no sign of Evan, but several cars dotted the spaces in front of the main doors. Normally employees, including the bank manager, would've readied the bank for business. Today, undercover officers had taken their places. It'd been risky to involve so many members of law enforcement—Evan may have been telling the truth about having eyes and ears inside the Knoxville Police Department—but protecting civilians had precedence.

Flowers lined the walkway to the front door. Kyle placed a hand between Sierra's shoulder blades to avoid drawing attention to the gun holstered at the small of her back. He was also carrying, with the addition of a knife on his belt and a backup gun strapped to his ankle.

The automatic doors to the bank slid open and a security guard greeted them with a nod. He wasn't someone Kyle recognized. An undercover cop? Tension knitted his muscles and he took a deep breath to loosen them. Adrenaline would narrow his vision and cause his hands to shake. Neither would be useful in a dangerous situation. His gaze swept the lobby.

Tucker was stationed behind one of the teller stations, his red beard freshly trimmed to match the professional atmosphere. Logan was typing on a computer in a nearby cubicle designed for loan officers. A door leading to the bank vault opened and another security guard entered the lobby. Kyle's pulse kicked up a notch as recognition slammed into him.

Agent Jeff Lewis.

What was he doing here? Chief Garcia hadn't shared information about this operation with the FBI. There was no way Jeff should've known about it. Was he working for Blackstorm? Or had Jeff learned about the secret operation and demanded to be a part of it? Either scenario was likely. Kyle's gaze dropped to the gun holstered at Jeff's waist before his attention swung back to the other security guard. A tattoo peeked out from under the collar of the man's uniform, and when he smiled, it didn't reach his eyes.

Agent Lewis strolled past Tucker's station, and the former Army Ranger's eyes widened briefly before a mask of indifference shuttered his expression. Clearly, no one knew the FBI agent was going to be here. Kyle's anxiety about the safety of their mission racketed up. Before he could alert Sierra, the doors to the bank swished open again. Evan, followed by Iris holding Daniel, stepped inside.

The hitman removed the glasses shielding his eyes and smirked. "Morning." Evan's attention drifted to Kyle and his mouth hardened. "I see you brought a bodyguard."

"You didn't expect me to come alone." Sierra jutted up her chin. "Give Daniel to Kyle. He'll hold him while we retrieve the evidence from the safe deposit box."

"Not a chance." Evan lifted the edge of his shirt, revealing a black vest underneath. "There's enough dynamite attached to me to scatter pieces of us from here to Austin." He showed them his other hand, which held a detonator, controlled by pushing a button on top. A smile stretched across Evan's face. "There are only two options here. I'm walking out of this bank with the evidence or we all die. I'm not going to prison."

Kyle's mouth went dry. He wasn't an expert on bombs, but he knew enough from his time overseas to recognize the truth about what Evan was saying. There were enough explosives attached to the hitman to destroy the bank, killing everyone inside.

TWENTY-SIX

Sierra raised her hands in the classic sign of surrender. Her heart thumped against her rib cage, the sound of her accelerated pulse roaring in her ears. Everything she loved most in this world was inside the bank. Kyle and Daniel.

Please, God, give me the right words.

"There's no need to threaten us." Her voice came out strong, belying the gripping fear making her knees weak. "We can all walk out of this alive. I'll do exactly as you say."

Evan smirked, dropping the edge of his shirt to cover the homemade bomb vest. "I figured you'd see it my way. First things first, get the evidence from the safe deposit box. The rest of us will wait right here for you."

Daniel fussed and Iris rocked him side to side. Sierra's brain couldn't make heads or tails of what her eyes were seeing. There wasn't a flicker of fear in the other woman's expression. Iris glanced up and must've read the confusion on Sierra's face because her lips curved into a smile. "I'm not going to prison either."

Evan laughed. "You miscalculated us, Jacqueline." His eyes glinted with hatred. "Get the evidence. Now."

She didn't have a choice. Sierra glanced at Kyle, and he nodded reassuringly. The man was braver than anyone she'd ever known. A hero. But even he couldn't stop Evan from blowing up everyone in the bank. Any move they made to disarm the hitman wouldn't be quick enough to prevent Evan from hitting the ignition button attached to his vest.

She turned, but Evan stopped her with a warning. "Two minutes. And don't think about alerting the police."

"I wouldn't dream of it." Feet heavier than lead, Sierra crossed the lobby to Tucker's window. Evan was close enough to hear their conversation, so she simply said, "I'd like to open my safe deposit box, please."

"Of course, ma'am." Tucker went through the motions of verifying her ID and then he escorted her to the rear of the bank. Once they were safely inside the vault, he shut the door. "What's wrong?"

"Evan has a bomb strapped to his body. He's threatening to blow up the entire bank." The words came out in a rush. "You need to message the rest of the team members. People need to get out of here."

He hesitated. "They can't do it in a way that'll tip Evan off."

Sierra recognized the wisdom of Tucker's words, but that didn't ease the panic slashing her insides. It clawed up her throat making it hard to pull in a full breath. She checked her watch. A minute had already passed since she left Evan. Was he counting from the time she went into the vault? Or from the time she started talking to Tucker? The latter was the safest assumption. "Hurry, Tucker. Evan's only given me two minutes to return with the evidence."

He pulled his phone from his pocket and sent a quick text, probably to Logan. Then he inserted the bank's key into the right safe deposit box. Sierra's fingers trembled so badly, she couldn't undo the latch holding her necklace so she broke the chain. The jeweled cross fell to the carpet. Her instinct was to retrieve it, but there wasn't a second to waste.

She shoved her key into the slot. At the same time, Sierra and Tucker unlocked the box. He removed it from the wall and set it on the table in the center of the room. She touched the cool metal and a fresh wave of fear washed over her. Her vision narrowed. What if the evidence wasn't inside? What if Lucy simply left another clue for her to follow?

"Sierra." Tucker's sharp voice cut through her fright.

Belatedly, she realized her breath was shallow and quick. She was hyperventilating, about to pass out. Sierra forced herself to take a deep inhale and let it out slowly. "I'm okay." She repeated the act and then flipped open the lid of the safe deposit box.

A set of flash drives rested on a stack of documents. Sierra glimpsed Lucy's handwriting on the top page. She quickly scanned the note as she snatched the drives. She kept one for herself and handed the other to Tucker for safekeeping.

Take this to the public. Don't rely on the authorities alone. I'm sorry, sis. I love you.

There was no time to process her sister's final words. A loud noise came from beyond the door and the floor underneath Sierra's feet vibrated. Her heart stopped.

That'd been a bomb.

No!

Sierra bolted for the door, ignoring Tucker as he screamed her name, and flung it open. Clouds of billowing smoke smacked her in the face. A hand reached out and grabbed her arm. The flash drive was ripped from her grasp and then she had a quick flash of a gun before it was raised toward Tucker.

She shoved the arm. The weapon fired, the explosion ringing in her ears. Then Sierra was being dragged through the bank toward the rear entrance at the back of the hall. Her throat seized as the thick smoke attacked her lungs. Her eyes teared, blinding her. Sierra could barely make out her attacker's form. He seemed to have something over his face. A mask? A gas mask?

She reached for the gun at the small of her back, but the man shoved her against the wall. Her head collided with the hard cement and fireworks exploded behind her eyes. The weapon was ripped from the holster, leaving her defenseless. The smoke mingled with the fear leaving a bitter taste in her mouth.

Once again, the masked man grabbed her arm with a bruising grip and dragged her down the hall. He hit the bar on a door and brilliant sunshine blinded Sierra. She coughed, doing her best to drag fresh air into her lungs. A van sat a short distance away. The attacker shoved and pushed her toward it.

She blinked, desperate to clear her vision, and the scene came into focus. Evan was behind the wheel of the vehicle. Iris was also inside, a car seat next to her. A tiny fist waved above the edge of the hard plastic.

Daniel. He was alive.

Her heart soared. Sierra was shoved the last several steps to the van and roughly lifted inside. She planted a foot in her attacker's gut and earned the satisfaction of hearing him grunt. It didn't last though. He swung hard, smacking her across the face with the back of his hand. Sierra's head jerked back as pain exploded across her cheek.

Iris cursed. "We don't have time for this. Get in the van."

Her voice snapped with authority. Had Sierra been wrong about her father being the leader of Blackstorm? He was involved, but the way Iris was behaving, maybe the FBI had been correct. It was too much to process all at once. Smoke billowed from the side of the bank and pieces of burned and twisted metal mingled with glass on the ground. A car bomb.

The man ripped off his mask. Sierra gasped.

Agent Jeff Lewis.

He climbed inside, kicking her legs out of the way. The sound of pounding footsteps came from beyond him. Someone gave a guttural war cry. "Sierra!"

Kyle. She scrambled to a sitting position on the floor of the van.

He was rounding the corner of the bank, clothes coated with ash and grime.

Jeff raised his weapon.

Sierra kicked out with her foot but wasn't fast enough. Jeff's gun exploded.

Evan smashed on the gas and the van door slammed closed. Sierra scrambled to her knees to look out the window. Horror and heartache slammed into her with full force. Kyle lay motionless on the ground, blood pooling around him.

Tires squealed as Evan rounded the side of the bank and flew into the street. Sierra was tossed like a rag doll against the back of the seat. Daniel cried out at the sudden jostling motion. His wail sliced through Sierra, dragging home the desperate position they were now in.

Prisoners. And at the Blackstorm leader's mercy.

Whoever that may be.

TWENTY-SEVEN

Sierra focused on taking one breath. Then another.

It was the only way to survive this. By keeping her emotions at bay and forcing her senses to stay alert. She needed to be prepared.

To escape. To fight.

The van's wheels ate up the miles, and she lost track of how long they'd been driving. Iris searched her for audio- or video-recording devices, but missed the GPS tracker in her shoe. Would it help? With so much chaos at the bank, Sierra wasn't sure anyone would find her in time.

Jeff swiped a hand through his hair and grinned. "Surprised to see me, huh?"

"Not as much as you think." Sierra met his gaze, unwilling to give him the pleasure of seeing her fear. "We suspected you from the beginning."

Evan laughed and punched Jeff in the shoulder. "Told ya."

"Shut up, both of you." Iris glared at the men before zeroing in on the FBI agent. "Jeff, where's the evidence?"

He handed over the flash drive. Her eyes glinted with satisfaction. "Finally. I knew once I started managing things myself, we'd get the job done."

The men were quiet in reply. Daniel must've fallen asleep because he didn't make a sound. Sierra kept racking her brain, trying to figure a way out of the situation. She could attack Evan, causing him to have a wreck, but Daniel might be hurt in the process. She could try to take down Iris, but there were also two men in the vehicle and they'd shoot her. Running once the vehicle stopped wasn't an option either. She wouldn't leave without Daniel.

The van slowed down and Evan turned. A guard at a wrought-iron gate waved them past. Sierra strained to see out the windshield, but from her position on the floor of the van, it wasn't easy. Thick foliage lined either side of the vehicle, and then suddenly disappeared, revealing a spectacular mansion. Spiral posts held up the second-story balcony. A fountain sat in the center of the circular drive, water spraying from the top of the mermaid's hands. Evan stopped the van but didn't kill the engine.

"Jeff, get rid of this vehicle," Iris ordered. "Evan, you're in charge of the woman. I'll take the baby."

She popped the sliding door open and removed Daniel's carrier from the base. Evan circled the van and grabbed Sierra. She debated struggling against his hold, but what was the point? She wanted to be wherever Daniel was. As they headed toward the front door, the van's engine roared and the tires squealed as Jeff headed back down the driveway toward the gate.

"Idiot," Iris muttered. "The FBI was stupid to hire him. He's not smart enough to tie his own shoes." She pushed open the front door, still grumbling. "I should shoot him myself. He's outlived his usefulness."

"I can do it." Evan smiled.

Bile rose in Sierra's throat as her stomach churned. They were discussing killing a man with the same dismissive tone someone might use to order a tuna sandwich. It was sickening. To calm her nerves, she kept her gaze on Daniel. Thank God, he looked perfectly fine. His eyes were closed in sweet slumber, long lashes resting on chubby cheeks. His nose didn't appear to be running, nor was his complexion flushed.

Evan manhandled Sierra down the expansive entryway and into an office. He pushed her onto a leather sofa. Iris set Daniel on the floor nearby and swiped a hand through her blond hair. A door opened behind Sierra. She twisted in her seat and her heart stuttered.

Cece strolled into the room. She was dressed in a designer pantsuit, diamond earrings dangling from her lobes. Her hair was curled into soft waves only a professional could accomplish. Behind her, Oliver followed. His face was a hard mask of indifference. He barely glanced at Sierra.

"Well, well, well. You've caused us quite a bit of trouble." Cece planted manicured hands on her hips. Her gaze was cold enough to turn water to ice. "Few people stay alive very long once I've given the order to have them killed."

Sierra smothered her surprise behind a quick inhale, but Cece caught it anyway. Her ruby lips curved into a cunning smile. "Yes, dear. I'm the leader of Blackstorm. Always have been." She flashed a look of adoration toward Oliver. "My husband has been working with me for decades as my right-hand man. After we're done taking care of this troubling business, we're going to raise Daniel as our own child."

Rage circled Sierra's fingers into fists. "You killed my sister and her husband."

"Your sister should've minded her own business." Cece turned to Iris and Evan. "Where's the evidence?"

Iris handed over the flash drive. Cece ordered them to leave the room before turning her full attention back to Sierra. "Is this the only copy?"

"Yes."

Cece glanced at her husband. Oliver stepped forward and yanked Sierra's hair. Pain screamed from her scalp as he twisted so hard she feared her neck would snap. He pressed a sharp blade against her throat. She froze as the knife pricked her skin. His breath was hot on her face, his expression menacing. "Tell the truth."

This. This was the man she remembered. Sierra trembled, unable to keep the fear from her voice. "I am. That's the only copy."

Oliver seemed to debate whether to believe her. Sierra forced herself to hold his gaze, as the sound of her pulse thumped against the edge of the blade. One move and he would slice her throat. Finally, he pulled the knife away and pushed her head with so much force, she nearly fell off the couch.

"She's telling the truth."

Sierra breathed out in silent relief. Her limbs trembled with exhaustion and stress. Daniel was still resting in his carrier, sleeping, completely oblivious to the danger swirling around them. She licked her dry lips and let her gaze drift around the immediate area. A flash of steel caught her attention under a pile of magazines on the side table. A knife? Possibly.

Cece handed her husband the flash drive. "Let's see what's on this."

"Of course, darling."

Oliver took it from her and circled the desk to fire up the computer. Cece went to stand behind him. Sierra used their momentary distraction to shift some magazines with her foot.

A letter opener.

It wasn't much, but it was something. Trouble was, she couldn't reach it without diving off the couch. Sierra needed to bide her time and wait for the right opportunity. Lights flickered behind the large window beyond Oliver and Cece. Sierra peered into the yard, trying to make sense of what she was seeing.

"This needs a password," Cece snarled. She turned toward Sierra. "What is it?"

Her mind momentarily glitched. Password? Lucy hadn't left her...the image of her sister's first letter popped into her mind. She'd included an address and the first 16 digits of pi. That had to be the password. Lucy was a genius.

The lights went out.

Shouts came from down the hall, followed by the sound of shattering glass. Sierra didn't wait for her eyes to become adjusted in the dark. She grabbed the letter opener from the side table and scooped up Daniel's carrier with the other hand. The open doorway leading to another part of the house was somewhere to her left but hard to distinguish in the pitch black. Someone banged into the desk, and by the sound of the curse that followed, it was Oliver.

A crash came from the window. Sierra ducked, her heart racing. She didn't know what was happening, but she prayed it was the police breaking in. That notion couldn't be relied on though. Considering Blackstorm's violent crimes, a rival organization could be attacking.

She wasn't taking chances. Not with Daniel to protect.

A bullet whizzed past her head. She yelped and started running, the doorway to the next room looming large as her eyes adjusted to the dim surroundings. A form stepped in front of her and Sierra attempted to skid to a stop but failed. Someone grabbed her arm and shoved her to the ground. Gunshots erupted. She threw herself over Daniel, desperate to protect him. He cried, startled by all the noise.

The sound of the gunshots faded. Daniel's wails continued. She took it as a good sign that he was unharmed. A commotion was happening in the next room, the conflicting sounds too difficult to make out. Sierra trembled, clutching the letter opener in her hand. The lights flickered and then came back on. She whirled, raising her weapon, prepared to use it on her attacker.

Her breath caught as his face came into focus.

Kyle.

He was dressed in all black. A pair of night-vision goggles dangled from one hand, a handgun from the other. His mouth curved into a handsome, heartbreaking smile. "Don't stab me, sweetheart. I'm here to save you."

Tears flooded her eyes. Sierra dropped the letter opener, and it clattered to the carpet. Then she threw herself into Kyle's arms. "You're okay. You're alive."

"The bullet grazed my head and knocked me out, that's all."

She shook her head in disbelief. Only Kyle would take a bullet to the head, get back up, and race in to rescue her. He was her knight in shining armor, if ever there was one. She planted a kiss on his lips before backing out of his arms to comfort Daniel. The infant was still crying, upset by all the commotion. She popped him out of his carrier and cuddled him close. He gave a last shaky cry before quieting down.

Inside the office, police had Oliver and Cece in handcuffs. Both of them had been shot and were receiving medical attention. Bullet holes were embedded in the wood near Sierra's head. She trembled. "They tried to kill me even as the house was being raided by the police."

"Cece did. She got a bullet for her trouble."

Kyle had saved her. Oliver caught sight of them and glared. He spat obscenities and struggled against the handcuffs and officers holding him down. She turned away, feeling nothing but pity and disgust. He was not her father. They might share DNA, but Sierra was nothing like him. "Cece is the leader of Blackstorm. Oliver has been working with her for decades."

"Both of them are going to prison for the rest of their lives." Kyle wrapped his arms around Sierra and Daniel. "Thank God you're both okay." He kissed the top of Sierra's head, letting out a shuddering breath. "I said a lot of prayers on the way over here."

"God heard you." She snuggled closer into his embrace and stared down at her nephew's sweet face. They were safe now. Forever. "He heard us both."

TWENTY-EIGHT

One week later

The backyard was full of people.

Kyle stood on the porch, a soft drink in his hand, and the scents of smoked BBQ tickling his nostrils. His father and Tucker were manning the grill, serving ribs and smoked brisket to the hungry crowd. Tables were scattered in the grass, music blasted from the speakers surrounding the picnic area, and a collection of pie boxes sat waiting for dessert time. Harriet and Nelson had shut the diner down for the afternoon to attend the event. The couple was chatting with Jason and Addison. From the looks of things, the party was a success.

A set of slender arms wrapped around Kyle's waist, embracing him from behind. "There you are. I was looking for you."

He turned and pulled Sierra closer before brushing his lips across hers. Kyle's heart skipped several beats, and he was tempted to deepen the kiss, but mindful of the fact that everyone at the party could see them. With regret, he kept it light.

She smiled, her whole face lighting up. It warmed his heart to see her so happy. Kyle tucked a loose strand of her hair behind one ear. "Are you having a good time?"

"Yep. It was a wonderful idea to throw a party for everyone." Amusement made her eyes twinkle. "Any chance I could talk you into a game of horseshoes?" Her mouth twitched. "Of course, if you'd rather not, I understand. It's difficult playing with the reigning champion."

"Oh, those are fighting words." He chuckled. "Careful, sweetheart. I've had a lot of practice since high school. You might lose your number-one spot."

She burst out laughing. "Never."

Someone cleared a throat nearby, and Kyle raised his head to find Chief Garcia, hat in hand, standing at the bottom of the porch. A blush crept across Sierra's cheeks, and she pulled away from Kyle, but he kept one arm around her shoulders. He enjoyed having her close. "Hey, Chief. Everything okay?"

"Fine. Better than fine, actually." He climbed the steps to join them on the porch. "I just got official news from the FBI and wanted to let y'all know immediately. Jeff Lewis was arrested an hour ago. Blackstorm is officially disbanded and every single one of the top leaders are in custody."

Kyle wanted to leap for joy. Sierra and Daniel were safe. Officially and completely. From the ecstatic look on Sierra's face, she was feeling the same way.

"Did the evidence Lucy uncover help with the investigation?" she asked.

"It was instrumental. That's the other piece of news I have for you. Iris sang like a canary once investigators presented her with the files. She's been working for Blackstorm for a long time, and her testimony aided the FBI in shutting the criminal organization down. Once Oliver and Cece realized Iris flipped on them, they accepted a plea deal. None of them, including Jeff, will ever see the outside of a prison cell." The chief gave Sierra a sympathetic look. "I know it doesn't bring Lucy back, but I hope it provides you with some measure of peace. She was a brave lady." His eyes warmed with affection. "Must run in the family."

Sierra chuckled. "It does." Her expression grew serious. "Was Iris the one who figured out what my sister was doing? Or was it Jeff?"

"It was Iris. No one in Blackstorm knew where you or your sister were hiding, so Iris was unaware of Lucy's true identity until after your sister started investigating Jackson Construction."

"She reported it to Oliver and Cece," Kyle surmised.

The chief nodded. "That's when they realized who Lucy really was. They flew into cleanup mode, part of which meant finding leverage on Jeff. On paper, he was clean, but according to his superiors, Jeff was unhappy with his position in the FBI. He wanted to move up the ranks higher and faster, to have more prestige and money." His expression darkened. "He betrayed his oath for a pile of cash, I'm sorry to say."

"The important thing is that we shut Blackstorm down." Sierra's eyes misted, and she squeezed Kyle's waist. "We're all safe and we got justice for Lucy. I'm very grateful."

"We all are." Kyle brushed a kiss across her head.

The chief echoed the sentiment. They exchanged a few more pleasantries, and then he excused himself to rejoin the party. The screen door creaked open and Gerdie appeared with Daniel. The baby had been napping. Kyle stopped his mom and scooped the little boy into his arms. "Someone's ready for a bottle."

Gerdie handed it over before also joining the party. Kyle settled on the porch swing next to Sierra to feed the baby. A sweet breeze danced over them, ruffling Sierra's hair. She had a pensive expression on her face.

"Penny for your thoughts?"

Her lips curved up into a small smile, and she ran a hand over Daniel's wild hair in an attempt to tame it. "I was just thinking about what my next step should be. Daniel and I stayed on the ranch for safety while the last members of Blackstorm were rounded up. Now that they are, it's time to return to regular life."

Kyle's chest clenched. They hadn't discussed their future since the raid, in part, because he recognized Sierra had been through something difficult and traumatic. She was also beginning the grief process for her sister. He didn't want to pressure her into making a decision about their relationship. At the same time, this last week with her and Daniel had been some of the best days of his life. They'd settled into a routine that was natural and loving. He never wanted them to leave.

"Actually..." His mouth went dry as a sudden fear gripped him. What if Sierra didn't want to stay? It would hurt, but he'd support her in whatever she wanted. Kyle swallowed hard. "I was hoping you and Daniel would stay here. With me."

Sierra inhaled sharply. Her gaze lifted to his face. "Do you mean that?"

"With all my heart." He removed the bottle from Daniel's lips and set it on a nearby table before tugging a jewelry box from his pocket. He'd purchased the engagement ring the day after the raid. Carefully, without jostling the baby, he got down on one knee. "I love you, Sierra. Daniel too. I want us to be a family. Will you marry me?"

Tears flooded her vision. Kyle tried to read her expression but couldn't. He stayed where he was. "You don't have to decide now, if it's too much. I know this is quick, and I understand if you don't feel the same way or aren't ready. It's okay. We can wait." He smiled reassuringly. "For you and Daniel, I'd wait forever."

Sierra swiped at the tears coursing down her cheeks. "You don't have to wait forever." Her voice was thick with emotion. "There's nothing I want more than to marry you."

Kyle's chest swelled with happiness. Sierra cupped his face and kissed him, her touch tender and full of promise. Daniel whimpered, breaking the moment, and they both immediately checked to make sure he was okay before laughing.

Sierra lightly touched the baby's back. "This is going to be our lives. Stolen kisses between moments of parenting."

"That sounds perfect." He wrapped an arm around her waist. She hadn't even had a chance to put on the ring yet, but that didn't matter. The most important things were encircled in his embrace, Sierra and Daniel.

His family.

ALSO BY LYNN SHANNON

Texas Ranger Heroes Series

Ranger Protection

Ranger Redemption

Ranger Courage

Ranger Faith

Ranger Honor

Triumph Over Adversity Series

Calculated Risk

Critical Error

Necessary Peril

Strategic Plan

Would you like to know when my next book is released? Or when my novels go on sale? It's easy. Subscribe to my newsletter at www. lynnshannon.com and all of the info will come straight to your inbox!

Reviews help readers find books. Please consider leaving a review at your favorite place of purchase or anywhere you discover new books. Thank you.